PUFFIN BOOKS

THE
DANGER
GANG

Also by Tom Fletcher
THE CHRISTMASAURUS
THE CREAKERS

BRAIN FREEZE
(written specially for World Book Day 2018)

For younger readers
THERE'S A MONSTER IN YOUR BOOK
THERE'S A DRAGON IN YOUR BOOK
THERE'S AN ALIEN IN YOUR BOOK
THERE'S AN ELF IN YOUR BOOK
THERE'S A SUPERHERO IN YOUR BOOK
THERE'S A WITCH IN YOUR BOOK

Written with Dougie Poynter, for younger readers
THE DINOSAUR THAT POOPED CHRISTMAS
THE DINOSAUR THAT POOPED A PLANET!
THE DINOSAUR THAT POOPED THE PAST!
THE DINOSAUR THAT POOPED THE BED!
THE DINOSAUR THAT POOPED A RAINBOW!
THE DINOSAUR THAT POOPED DADDY!
THE DINOSAUR THAT POOPED A PRINCESS!
THE DINOSAUR THAT POOPED A PIRATE!

THE DINOSAUR THAT POOPED A LOT!
(written specially for World Book Day 2015)

Written with Giovanna Fletcher, for older readers
EVE OF MAN
THE EVE OF ILLUSION

THE DANGER GANG

TOM FLETCHER

Illustrations by Shane Devries

PUFFIN

PUFFIN BOOKS

UK | USA | Canada | Ireland | Australia
India | New Zealand | South Africa

Puffin Books is part of the Penguin Random House group of companies
whose addresses can be found at global.penguinrandomhouse.com.

www.penguin.co.uk   www.puffin.co.uk   www.ladybird.co.uk

First published 2020
001

Set in Baskerville MT Pro
Text design by Mandy Norman
Printed in Great Britain by Clays Ltd, Elcograf S.p.A.

A CIP catalogue record for this book is available from the British Library

HARDBACK
ISBN: 978–0–241–40733–2

INTERNATIONAL PAPERBACK
ISBN: 978–0–241–40755–4

All correspondence to:
Puffin Books, Penguin Random House Children's
One Embassy Gardens, 8 Viaduct Gardens, London SW11 7BW

*In memory of Neil Tierney, who
led our Danger Gang on some
truly unforgettable adventures.*

MEET THE DANGER GANG

FRANKY BROWN,
the hero of this tale!

ERIC FLIPPERSON,
who's a little dangerous
when wet . . .

KATY SPECK,
who's small but mighty!

JAMELIA POINTER,
who's braver than she thinks.

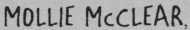

MOLLIE McCLEAR,
who's quiet but awesome.

SUZY PRUNE,
who's got a lot of
GROWING UP to do.

**CHARLIE
CAMPBELL,**
who **LOVES**
scary creatures!

RONNIE NUTBOG,
who's nice underneath it all . . .

CONTENTS

PROLOGUE
THE STORM

The lightning was green and smelled of poo.

I know that might not be the best way to start a book, but it's the truth. Besides, I want you all to know right away that this story is a little bit *gross*.

A little bit *strange*.

A little bit *unusual*.

And it all started on a

dark and
stormy night . . .

OK. Storms aren't that unusual, but this one was different. Just like this story, it was a little bit *gross*.

A little bit *strange*.

A little bit *unusual*.

And not just because it smelled like a dog's bottom, but because *this* storm wasn't natural.

It happened above a quiet, sleepy street in a quiet, sleepy town. The deep green clouds puffed and swelled angrily like an avalanche in the sky, hiding the stars and blotting out the night, leaving only a tiny gap for the eerie full moon to stare through.

A flash of bright green lit up the darkness, followed by a rather eggy pong wafting across the sleeping houses in Strike Lane. Then came the thunder, rumbling through the sky, followed swiftly by the rain.

It poured down in buckets on to the rooftops and gardens, drenching the plants and soaking the socks of the people who had left their washing on the line – for no one had expected this storm.

FLASH!

Another bolt of green lightning struck, zapping a tall tree and sending sparks showering down on to the wet pavement below, electrifying the street.

Now we all know that lightning storms can be scary at the best of times, but if you'd seen this one you would have run to your bedroom, buried your head under your pillow and possibly even done a little wee in your PJs.

Don't believe me? Ask Franky. He was there. (He didn't wee in his PJs, though. At least, he promises he didn't.)

He watched the storm through his kitchen window. He heard the mighty crash of thunder, saw the lightning bolts zap the houses, charging them with mysterious green energy . . . What Franky didn't see was how that weird energy was transforming some of the people inside as they slept.

Franky had only just moved to this freaky town – Oh yes – I forgot to say! That was its name:

FREAKY.

You've never heard of it? Well, I can't say I'm surprised. People don't really like to talk about Freaky. It gives folks the **heebie-jeebies**,

the spooky-wookies,

the shivery-quivers,

the shuddery-wudderies . . .

OK, I might have made that last one up, but the long and the short of it is that people feel a bit uneasy if they think you come from Freaky.

Why?

Because weird things are **known** to happen in Freaky.

If you're wondering where this totally real, not-made-up-at-all place is, then I can tell you. It's just outside London. You can even get there on the Tube if you want. It's two stops past Strange, and if you get to Bonkers you've gone much too far!

Freaky hasn't always been the way it is today. It used to be so un-freaky you might even have gone as far as to call it 'normal'. The thing is, a book about a normal town would be as boring as **watching paint dry**. Brown paint! Brown paint on a wall that was already brown, but just a bit faded and needed retouching! A faded brown wall in the toilet of an accountant's office! No one would ever want to read a book about that.

Wait, what was *this* book about again?

Oh yes! FREAKY!

Well, I'm afraid to say that if it hadn't been for Franky moving there, the situation might not have ended up quite so . . . freaky.

I'm not saying it was *all* his fault, but, if Franky hadn't asked his dad to order that delicious cheesy pizza for dinner on the night of the strange storm, things would have turned out very differently.

The stupidest thing of all is that he would have got away with it if he hadn't *written the WHOLE THING down*.

Here's a bit of free advice: if something ever goes wrong and you're to blame . . .

DON'T WRITE IT DOWN!

(You'll thank me for that one day.)

Remember I said that Franky was new to Freaky? Well, when Franky moved to Freaky, he didn't really mind leaving his old town behind. As far as he was concerned, a town was a town, a school was a school and a park was a park. He'd have all those things in Freaky. But the one thing he *wasn't* going to have was his best friend, Danika.

Yeah, that's right. Franky's best friend was a girl. I know what you're thinking, and the answer is **NO**. She wasn't his girlfriend. That's what everyone used to think, but they were just best mates.

Honest . . .

Don't look at me like that!

Friends.

Best friends.

Nothing more.

Got it?

OK.

Franky and Dani did **everything** together. They loved climbing the highest trees and practising mega-wheelies on their bikes (although Dani's were always better, even though Franky would never admit that!). They were fascinated by absolutely anything to do with space and loved staying up to spot satellites orbiting the Earth (they look like moving stars!). They liked the same zombie movies, the same comic books, the same nutter-crunch ice cream, the same triple-fudge doughnuts. They both loved Franky's mum's spaghetti and meatballs, Dani's dad's super-spicy chicken, and takeaway pizza with extra-extra cheese. And they

LOVE,

LOVE,

LOVED

the Zack Danger: Super-Spy books. They were having a competition to see who could read the whole series first and were both official members of the Zack Danger fan club: the Danger Gang, for kids who wanted to be super-spies themselves one day.

And they always had each other's back.

Like the time Franky got flu and had to stay home from school. Dani pretended she was sick too and sneaked in through his bedroom window, using the ladder from Franky's garden shed, and they watched zombie movies all day. (Including *Attack of the Killer Kittens Part 2*. The *really* scary one their parents didn't want them to see!)

That backfired when Dani caught the flu for real. Her mum said she'd been sick for too long so must be faking it now and made her go to school.

Plus, Franky had nightmares for three weeks about the killer kittens.

Franky and Dani were like chips and ketchup. Chips are all right on their own, and ketchup goes with pretty much anything, but nothing beats them both together. So Franky knew that moving to a new town without Dani was going to be tough. That's why he decided to start writing letters to her.

No, they were **NOT** love letters!

After that stinky storm, when things started getting seriously weird in Freaky, he *had* to tell his best friend about it.

That's why everything that happened was written down and it's time for you to read Franky's letters from

Freaky now. To discover the truth about that storm, and all that followed.

So get ready to uncover the secrets of the place, of the people and of . . .

THE DANGER GANG!

JANUARY

Dear Dani,

MOVING SUCKS.

This morning I packed the last of my Zack Danger books into the last flimsy cardboard box and said goodbye to my bedroom in Greyville. I know Greyville's just a regular town but as soon as this day came I really didn't want to leave. And I guess my stuff didn't want to leave either . . .

I told Mum that the hole in the box was a sign that we shouldn't go ahead with the move.

'Franky Brown,' she told me, not even looking up as she scribbled **KITCHEN** on the side of a box with a big felt-tip pen, 'I am a scientist. I only believe in fact-based evidence. Now hurry up! The removal van is going to be here soon.'

So I went and told Dad about the sign, but he just agreed with Mum, like he always does.

I walked out of my bedroom for the very last time. I didn't even shed a single tear like you said I would. And you know what that means, right? You owe me your limited-edition Zack Danger badge! You know, the super-awesome one that *looks* like a plain red badge, until you tilt it just right and the words **THE DANGER GANG** appear!

Oh man, I've loved that badge ever since the moment it fell out of that box of Danger Flakes Spy Cereal and landed in your bowl and not mine. And now it belongs to me! You can put it in the envelope when you write back. (YOU'D BETTER WRITE BACK, DANI!)

Dad says the new people moving in are going to turn my room into a gym. A GYM!

Can you believe that? I grew up in that room! We've had so many epic historic moments in there, Dani. It made me think of when we went on that school trip to London and we stopped to take photos of a blue plaque on the wall of a house, just because some author I'd never even heard of wrote a book there. Well, if that Dickens guy got a plaque just for writing some words down, then my bedroom deserves a plaque too. In fact, I thought I'd make one before I left so the new owners would know whose room it was they were working out in.

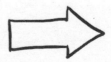

> **FRANKY BROWN**
> Picked <u>10,000</u> Bogies
> in THIS room
> from Age 0-10

The trouble is, Dad got suspicious when I asked which box he'd packed the hammer in, so I didn't get a chance to hang it up.

Seriously, though, we did SO many awesome things in there. We completed our first video game, saw our **FIRST UFO** through that window, and there was that time we spotted the same shooting star and my hand ACCIDENTALLY brushed yours and you thought I was trying to hold your hand. **HAHA! AS IF! YUCK!**

My cot was even in there when I was a baby. And now some stranger is going to fill it up with treadmills and rowing machines.

Well, I left them a note on the floor that I think might change their mind.

This is a __LEGAL DOCUMENT__ to certify that this __BEDROOM__ still belongs to a Mr Franky A. Brown. By reading this LEGAL DOCUMENT, you are entering a visual contract with Mr Franky A. Brown (the legal owner of said room) and agreeing that you __WILL NOT__ turn this historical landmark into a GYM and that you will instead get a gym membership like everyone else. Nor shall you change said bedroom in any way without written consent from Mr Franky A. Brown himself. If you break this contract, you will face serious ~~consekwen consecwens~~ you will be in big trouble with the LAW, including the police or worse — a LAWYER!

Unfortunately, Mum found the note before we left. 'You need to learn to let go of things, Franky,' she sighed.

'I'd happily leave Max behind,' I told her, but apparently that wasn't an option, so Max had to come with us to the new house too. This sucked because he pooped his nappy in the car on the way there, but Dad said there wasn't time to stop at the services, so I had to go the whole journey with my head out of the window to stop myself breathing in his poo particles.

We drove past that big cooking-apple tree in Mr Flaxson's front garden and I remembered the time I dared you to climb all the way to the top. When you did, you celebrated so hard the branch SNAPPED and you fell all the way down, landed on ME, and we both ended up in hospital with matching head bumps. We got to stay home from school together the next day though, which was pretty cool!

Then we ate that nutter-crunch ice cream we found right at the bottom of the freezer that was ten years out of date, because you said it was 'vintage' and that 'ice cream gets better with age' like the stinky cheese my dad eats at Christmas.

We both ended up with BRAIN FREEZE... AND FOOD POISONING.

PUKE!

Anyway, it made me realize that we'd done a lot of cool stuff together in Greyville. But Mum's really excited about the new job we're moving house for. 'I've wanted to be Head of Science for years, Franky. It's not every day these teaching jobs come up, you know!' she keeps saying. 'Plus, there's a big garage at the new house. Perfect for storing my work!'

So that's that.

But don't worry – I won't forget you.

WE'VE BEEN BEST FRIENDS FOREVER!

Which is why I thought I'd start writing you letters. It was actually my dad's idea, on the drive to the new house.

'You should try writing to Dani! I used to write to a French pen pal when I was a kid. His name was Jean-Claude. He used to love helicopters,' he remembered, starting one of his long stories about *when he was a kid* . . . so I zoned out after that.

LETTERS? AS IF! We both know letters are the most boring thing since dust, so I thought it was a totally rubbish idea, just like all my dad's other totally rubbish ideas.

'Yeah, no, it's a totally rubbish idea,' I told him. 'I'm just going to email Dani.'

But then I remembered that you share a computer with the supreme leader of PLANET ANNOYING – your older sister, and she always seems to be able to work out your passwords. Plus, we both know that Mya has had it in for me since day one!

PLANET ANNOYING

Then it hit me that writing letters is actually perfect! No one reads letters any more, so Mya will never be expecting it. And our parents will just be happy we're practising our handwriting.

(I once heard Mum say that Dad might actually be a genius if he wasn't such an idiot, and that it's a fine line. I think she might be right.)

So I'm going to write to you once a month to tell you what I've been getting up to in . . . Wait, I've just realized something. I haven't even told you the **ONLY** good thing about moving to this house! The town I'm moving to is called . . .

Can you believe it?! That's its actual name. I now live in Freaky! I'm writing you a letter from Freaky! It's a Freaky letter! I know, right? You couldn't make this stuff up!

UH-OH! I've got to go. Dad's ordered pizza for our first meal in the new house, and I want to see if the new delivery place is any good. I'll be back to finish this letter in a bit and to tell you what **FREAKY** pizza is like! That's never gonna get old!

I'M BACK! Freaky Pizza was all right. They could do with adding more cheese (you know I need **LOADS** of cheese on my pizza!), but the fact that the pizza place was actually called Freaky Pizza kind of makes up for it.

COOL NAME!

NOT ENOUGH CHEESE!

So I bet you're wondering about my new house. Number 13, Strike Lane. Another cool name, right? Well, unfortunately, that's all that is cool about it. Mum said this 'new' house was going to be **WAY** better than our old one, but when she showed me photos it looked like it smelled of mushrooms and, surprise, it does! Plus, there's nothing 'new' about it. When you get new clothes, they haven't already been worn by an old lady, so I don't see why we had to move to a house that had already been lived in by one (along with her eleven cats).

The front door has this weird, colourful glass in it, like the kind you find in churches. It looks nice, I guess, if you're into that sort of thing. I said it would be cooler if we had one of those ZOMBIE-PROOF front doors that can withstand the force of an undead army attack, but Mum said not to be so ridiculous – we could never afford one of those.

We've got all the usual stuff you'd expect to find in a house: a living room, kitchen, bedrooms, doors, windows, lights . . . And just off the kitchen is a huge garage – which is Mum's. Remember I said that was one of the main reasons we moved here? Well, Mum's wanted a place to store all her INVENTIONS for ages, and now she's got one. The rest of us have to KEEP OUT!

I suppose Mum being an INVENTOR is pretty cool, but I'll tell you this: when it comes to moving house, inventors are a

NIGHTMARE.

All her inventions need 'recalibrating' or something, which I think means they've all gone a bit loopy on the drive over here.

THE PANCAKE-O-MATIC started making stacks of pancakes when Mum unpacked the kitchen stuff, and it wouldn't stop!

Then the PANCAKE-O-MATIC flipped them out of the window. Well, it would have done if the WINDOW-OPEN-UPPER had been working properly, but unfortunately it was busy opening the downstairs toilet door instead!

And, worst of all, the AUTO-NAPPY-CHANGER can't seem to tell the difference between me and Max . . .

But, once Mum irons out all the bugs, things should go back to normal. Which reminds me: the ROBO-IRON decided to iron my shoes, but since I've got flat feet Dad thinks they should still fit me OK.

Anyway, there's one thing this house has that my old one didn't:

A BASEMENT!

I tried to get Mum and Dad to let me have it as my bedroom, but Dad said it was going to be his 'man cave'. The only other grown-up I know that has his own cave is Batman, so at first I thought Dad might be living some sort of secret DOUBLE LIFE as a superhero like Zack Danger, which would explain why he's such a nerd in everyday life. I couldn't wait to see what sort of secret superhero HQ he was going to install in this *man cave* in the basement!

You can imagine my disappointment when Mum explained that it was just a place for Dad to keep all his junk that she wouldn't let him have in the rest of the house. I think, because Mum gets to take over the garage, Dad decided he needed his own Dad-space too. He's so needy, but he's pretty chuffed that he got a man cave. There's no Bat-suit or gadgets, but he does have the brown armchair that our old dog chewed to bits (RIP, Billy), a dartboard and a tiny fridge full of fizzy drinks that I'm not allowed to have because Mum says they'll rot my teeth (Dad's teeth must be beyond hope).

WASTE. OF. SPACE.

So, instead of my Basement Bedroom of Dreams, I've got to climb two flights of rickety stairs to the top floor. And it's as spooky as it sounds.

'Up here you can make as much noise as you like, Franky!' Mum said, *really* trying to sell it to me.

'You'll be able to practise your drums without disturbing anyone!' Dad added. Dad loves that I've started playing an instrument – maybe he's hoping I'll be an out-of-work musician one day too. But I'd bet that awesome DANGER GANG badge you owe me that playing my drums at 3 a.m. is still going to be 'unacceptable'.

So what's my room like? Will it be blue-plaque-worthy? Well, imagine the SCARIEST,

MOST-DEFINITELY-HAUNTED ROOM YOU CAN THINK OF.

TIMES IT BY TWENTY AND ADD A MILLION!

Creaky floorboards: CHECK! ☑

Wardrobe doors that don't close all the way so the 'thing' living inside can watch you: CHECK!! ☑

Cold draught that comes in through the tiny cracks around the windows: CHECK!!! ☑

IT'S SAFE TO SAY THAT MY BEDROOM SUCKS.

I thought I'd make it a bit cosier by sticking up those glow-in-the-dark stars that were on the ceiling of my old room. You know, the ones we used to rearrange to spell funny words.

But guess what? My new bedroom is so dusty that they won't even stay up there. Mum told me to use the **DUST-O-MATIC** to clean it and then the stars should stick better, but with her inventions behaving in such a bonkers way I'm not touching them. And we both know the chances of me doing the dusting myself are zero. So that's why all my glow-stars are in the envelope with this letter, so you can put them on your ceiling. Maybe, when you're in bed looking at them, you can think of me in my haunted room in the house that smells of mushrooms and cats with the flimsy, non-zombie-proof front door.

I'll write again next month . . . if I'm still alive. Oh, when you walk past my old house on the way to school, try to see what they're doing inside. I want details!

FRANKY A. BROWN

PS Sorry for the X – I got carried away.

YUCK. LOL.

FEBRUARY

Dear Dani,

IT WORKED! You got my first letter! And you wrote back!! Did you notice that I used my mum's label machine to write your address on the envelope, just in case the supreme leader of Planet Annoying (your big sister) recognized my handwriting and ripped it up? Or, worse, **READ IT!**

Mya is such a nosy-face that her face might as well just be one big nose with two eyes, a mouth, then another nose right in the middle.

Anyway, your letter arriving makes up for today being <u>LAME</u>. Although I'm a bit worried that our new postman might be a thief, because the envelope **DID NOT** contain the DANGER GANG badge that

<u>YOU OWE ME!</u>

I guess there's a chance that Max ate it, because when the post fell through the letterbox he managed to waddle over and chew it all before Mum and Dad could get to him. I'm sure he must be half toddler, half dog, but Mum said that's not possible and he's just going through a **BITEY PHASE**.

If there *was* anything in your letter, I'm sure Dad will find it in his nappy sooner or later. Just like when he

swallowed my Zack Danger action figure's spy gun. (Max, not Dad!) I looked for that thing for ages before Max squeezed it out.

Thanks for checking up on my old house for me. I **CANNOT BELIEVE** the new owners have already taken down my treehouse!

THE FORTRESS OF FRANKY!

THE FRANK CAVE!

FRANKY AND DANI HQ!

THE DANGER GANG!

THAT PLACE WAS OUR HIDEOUT.

OUR SECRET LAIR.

What harm would it have done them to leave it? I knew I should have included it in the legal document I left them. Too late now. You live and learn. (Dad always says that. I'm not really sure what it means, but I think I've used it correctly.)

We've got a pretty good tree in our new garden though, and I've already got some big ideas for a Danger Gang HQ that will put our old one to shame. I've taken the liberty of drawing up some plans. Let me know what you think.

SPYCAM

TOYS

PIZZA PHONE WITH DIRECT
LINE TO FREAKY PIZZA

SLUSHY
MACHINE

FIREMAN'S
POLE

← DEATHSLIDE
INTO PLUNGE
POOL (NO SHARKS)

PRETTY COOL, RIGHT? It's a work in progress, but you live and learn. (That didn't sound right that time . . .)

How are things back in Greyville? I've got **SO** much to tell you about Freaky, especially my new school, Freaky Primary. It's pretty cool, except for one person:

RONNIE NUTBOG.

When I turned up at the school gates on my **VERY FIRST DAY**, Ronnie Nutbog was waiting for me. 'I heard there was a new kid starting today,' he grunted at me. 'Let's see if you've got anything good in your lunchbox.'

Obviously, I'm not scared of anyone and normally I'd have told him to shove off, but Ronnie Nutbog is

TWICE AS BIG AS ME

(which means that he's probably **THREE** times as big as you!).

Well, luckily for me, my dad had been on lunch duty that morning, and you know how useless he is at that kind of thing, so I had weird, stinky egg sandwiches. When Ronnie caught a whiff of those, he nearly threw my lunchbox on the floor and I thought he MIGHT leave me alone.

Unluckily for me, though, Mum had sneaked in a triple-fudge doughnut underneath the stinky sandwiches, along with a note saying:

GOOD LUCK ON YOUR FIRST DAY!
I'll be in the science classroom
if you need anything!!!

xxx

Ronnie crumpled up the note, shoved the

DELICIOUS, SQUIDGY DOUGHNUT

into his mouth and gave me a huge fudgy grin. 'Thanks, BUMFACE!' he mumbled as he wandered off, and a load of kids standing close by laughed.

I'm still pretty sad about that doughnut.

In my first class, instead of doing my work, I wrote a poem about Ronnie on my pencil case.

It's a new pencil case that I got for my first day of school. I know that might sound kind of lame, but this is no ordinary pencil case. It's one of my mum's inventions.

I'll draw it for you:

It has all these cool secret compartments and bits that flip open to reveal other secret compartments. There's a little detachable spoon for my yoghurt at lunchtime, the zip becomes a torch when you press it, it floats on water, it's fireproof, glows in the dark and there's even an emergency whistle! I mean, Mum went a bit overboard, to be honest, but when she said, 'Pencil cases are so expensive these days. It would be cheaper to MAKE one,' I didn't expect her to ACTUALLY DO IT.

This is the poem I wrote on the side of it. (Don't worry – the pencil case also comes with a fade-away spy pen, which means my POEMS top-secret messages on the side of it will disappear before my enemies can read them.)

Ronnie is a great big bumhead
With a face like a wrinkly bum
And a bum on his chin and two bums for eyes
And a bum for a dad and a mum.

He's got a bum nose
And a bum for a mouth
And there's something I must have forgotten . . .
Ah yes, it's his brain (which is very, very small)
And is not in his head – it's in his bottom!

I was really happy with that poem. But then my new teacher, Miss Tinky (that's her *actual* name!), saw that I'd been writing on my pencil case – and **NOT** writing about the Ancient Egyptians like she'd asked – so she came over to see what I'd been doing . . . and gave me a **SAD FACE** sticker on the class chart, which at Freaky Primary is **THE WORST**.

AND RONNIE NUTBOG LAUGHED.
(I don't like Ronnie Nutbog.)

Then it was hometime.

As if starting a new school wasn't embarrassing enough, because we moved house in January everyone in my class already knew each other and I realized that first impressions were everything. I had to play it cool, especially after the bad start with Ronnie Nutbog. The **LAST** thing I wanted was for my classmates to find out that my **MUM** is the **NEW SCIENCE TEACHER** or my life would be over. No one wants to hang out with a teacher's kid!

I was actually pretty grateful that Ronnie had crumpled up the note Mum had left in my lunchbox!

Luckily, my class don't have science on Mondays, so I managed to get through the whole first day without anyone finding out, until hometime – when Mum

CAME TO <u>MY</u>
CLASSROOM
TO <u>COLLECT</u> ME!

Everyone saw her waving at me through the window with her shiny new STAFF MEMBER name badge on her chest.

'Why is the new teacher waving at you?' a kid named Eric Flipperson asked curiously.

I shrugged and kept my head down.

'Is she your mum?' a girl called Suzy Prune asked.

'NO!' I spluttered.

'Wait, she is! I saw you moving into Number Thirteen over the weekend! You live on the same street as me! I live at Number Seven, the one with the yellow door,' another girl named Jamelia Pointer said.

All I could do was grab my bag and make a run for it.

But it was no use. It turns out that, as well as Jamelia Pointer, a bunch of kids in my class

LIVE ON THE SAME STREET AS ME!

There's Suzy Prune and Eric Flipperson, Katy Speck, Mollie McClear, Charlie Campbell and – this is the worst – Ronnie Nutbog. And they ALL saw me and the 'science teacher' walking home together!

Mollie McClear gave me a little wave as we went inside our houses, and I think Jamelia smiled, but across the road Ronnie Nutbog was laughing his head off as he went into Number 14.

FRANKY'S MUM'S A TEACHER!
FRANKY'S MUM'S A TEACHER!

IT WAS **SO** LAME.

I mean, I didn't cry or anything, but I was really miffed with Mum, especially when she started waving to them all like some sort of celebrity. But when we got home she pulled out a jumbo packet of marshmallows from her bag and said, 'Well done on your first day at school, Franky.' Then she let me eat the whole lot and, just like magic, the marshmallows somehow melted my crossness at Mum.

Anyway, today has totally taken over as my very worst day at Freaky Primary so far.

You know what today is, right?

VALENTINE'S DAY!

YUCK!

As if Valentine's Day isn't bad enough *already*, Miss Tinky made us ALL write stupid Valentine's Day cards in class. She said we could write to ANYONE IN THE CLASS or, if we didn't want to do that, we could write one to our mum or dad.

Everyone laughed when she said that, so there was *no way* I was going to send one to my parents. But there wasn't anyone in the class I wanted to send a shiny pink card with an even shinier, pinker love heart on the front.

I thought really hard about who would be the least embarrassing person in the class to send my card to, just in case they figured out it was me that sent it. I must have thought about it for longer than I realized, as before I knew it the lesson was nearly over and I hadn't written a thing!

I looked around at the other kids I could potentially send a card to. The list of NO WAY went on and on, but the clock was ticking and everyone was licking their envelopes already. So I panicked and wrote my card to the next person that popped into my head . . .

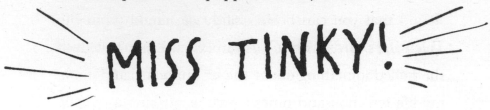

MISS TINKY!

GREAT IDEA! I thought. That saved the weird embarrassment of sending one of the girls in class a lovey-dovey, wishy-washy Valentine's Day card.

Everyone else had finished theirs so I quickly scribbled her name on the envelope and went to post it in the shiny red postbox that Miss Tinky had set up at the front of the class.

That's when Miss Tinky said,

'FRANKY BROWN, SINCE YOU'RE
THE LAST ONE UP, YOU CAN
HAND OUT ALL THE CARDS!'

'WHAT?!' I blurted.

'I said that you can be in charge of handing out the Valentine's cards. You're our class Cupid!' she trilled, as she pulled something out of the art cupboard and made my life ten thousand times worse by sticking a pair of home-made ANGEL WINGS on my back.

Well, you can imagine my **HORROR** as all those eyes watched me pick up the red box and start handing out the cards . . .

Two for Daisy Jacobs.

One for Jamelia Pointer.

RONNIE NUTBOG GOT THREE.

THREE Valentine's Day cards (which I'm pretty sure he sent to himself)!

I hand-delivered the sealed envelopes dressed as stupid Cupid and realized that I was nearly at the end of the box, which meant MY CARD was coming up soon.

There was no way of getting out of it now. I was going to have to hand a Valentine's card to Miss Tinky! But then she'd probably think it was from one of the goody-goody kids who sit at the front and get top marks in all their tests, or maybe even Ronnie Nutbog, trying to make up for getting caught eating chewie-chews in maths earlier. Either way, she'd never suspect it was from me, right?

I pulled out the card with my scribbled handwriting on the envelope and nervously approached Miss Tinky's desk.

'What's this?' Miss Tinky said, looking shocked. 'Is that a Valentine's Day card for *me*?'

'It appears to be, miss!' I said, pretending to look surprised to throw everyone off the scent. The whole class giggled as she took the red envelope.

'Well, I must say, this is a shock! No student has *ever* sent a teacher a Valentine's Day card before. What a shame it won't say who it's from. I'll *never* know who sent it!'

THAT'S WHEN MY HEART STOPPED.

THE WORLD SPUN.

AND I FELT SICK.

I suddenly realized that in my frantic hurry to write out the card I had TOTALLY FORGOTTEN that you are NOT supposed to write your name in Valentine's Day cards – and

I HAD SIGNED IT WITH MY FULL NAME!

DEAR MISS TINKY

WILL YOU BE MY VALENTINE?

FROM

Franky A. Brown

'Oh! Thank you very much, Franky A. Brown!' Miss Tinky trilled at the top of her lungs, spinning the card round so that EVERYONE COULD SEE.

The whole class burst out laughing, making kissing sounds. Ronnie Nutbog even made up a rhyme about us that went:

> *'Franky and Miss Tinky*
> *Sitting in a tree*
> *K-I-S . . . S . . . S . . . I . . . Q . . . T?'*

It's a good job that twerp can't spell or it would have been super embarrassing.

WORST DAY
IN FREAKY SO FAR!

Other than that, school's OK. Ronnie Nutbog still treats me like a bad smell or something. I used some of Dad's Bold Spice spray in case I *did* smell bad. Just a little squirt under my arms like he does in the morning, and I'll tell you right now: I am never using that stuff again! The rash stung so badly I couldn't lift my arms for a week, which made PE **REALLY TRICKY**!

You live and learn. (That felt right. Am I using that right?)

The other kids on my street – Mollie, Eric, Jamelia, Katy, Charlie and Suzy – seem pretty nice, although I've not really made any *proper* friends yet. But that's OK. I'm at school to learn. Not to make friends.

PAH-HA-HA!!!

I guess I'm still **THE TEACHER'S KID**. Although they'll realize soon enough that my mum isn't JUST a science teacher but an awesome inventor too. I mean, as soon as they see our home-made solar-powered family car that she invented, I bet they'll all be banging on the door and wanting to hang out with me.

I KEEP TELLING MUM TO MAKE IT FLY!
A hovercar would be **SO** awesome and I know she could totally do it. Dad says we wouldn't need to pay something called 'road tax' then, because technically we wouldn't be using the road, but Mum says there are better things to invent than hovercars.

AS IF!

FRANKY'S TOP THREE
THINGS MUM SHOULD INVENT

- HOVERCAR
- HOVERBOARD
- HOVERBIKE

I have a huge list of super-awesome stuff for her to invent for me, including those anti-gravity boots I've been banging on about for over a year.

BUT NO!

No anti-grav boots (YET). Not even hover-slippers! Just a pencil case. (OK, the pencil case *is* pretty cool.)

Mum *does* invent super-awesome stuff, but she keeps it hidden away in her **HSL**. (**H**ome **S**cience **L**ab. Which is just a fancy-pants name for the garage.)

GARAGE

H.S.L.

It's cool having a real science lab in our house, but the rules are pretty lame.

MUM'S HOME SCIENCE LAB RULES
DANGER!!!

- The HSL is off limits to everyone except Mum.
- This is not a garage: it is a scientific research centre.
- No children, no toddlers and no husbands in the HSL! Scientists only!

This only makes the garage – sorry, the HSL – even more tempting for me, Dad and Max. We try to get sneak peeks of what she's working on whenever she leaves the door open.

I'M NOT SUPPOSED TO TELL YOU THIS BUT . . .

Well, I guess there's no harm in it. You know that I said my mum had a really boring job for a really boring company where she had to invent really boring inventions . . . like the nose-hair dryer for people with really long nose hair, and the ironing-board treadmill for people who like to walk while they iron, or, even worse, the dinner plate that's always dirty for people who love doing the washing-up . . . Well, that was a lie. I made all that up. Sorry. The truth is, before we moved to Freaky, Mum used to work for this top-secret science company back in Greyville, called **SHADOW TECH** (cool name, right?!). She invented loads of really awesome stuff for them that she said we're all going to have in the future, like the **LUGGAGE SHRINK-O-ZAP** that can shrink your suitcase at the airport so that everyone can take as much as they want on holiday.

Mum had that idea when we went to Spain last year and one of our suitcases was too heavy so Dad had to take some stuff out. Unfortunately, when he opened the zip, the case

ExPLODED

and fired Mum's **KNICKERS** all over Terminal One.

Or the **KID-SHUTTER-UPPER**, which was another zapping laser that keeps children quiet for five minutes. Mum got that idea on the same holiday.

ARE WE THERE YET? . . .
ARE WE THERE YET? . . .
ARE WE THERE YET?!

ZAP!

This invention was shortly followed by the **HUSBAND-O-SHHHH** ('*the wonder machine that will turn your husband into a SHUSHband*'), which basically does the same thing, but it only works on husbands and the silencing effects **LAST FOR A WHOLE HOUR!**

Mum had to dismantle that one though, as the temptation to use it was too great for her to handle responsibly. That's what Dad said anyway (when Mum wasn't listening).

And I can tell you all this now because Mum got fired from that job with **SHADOW TECH**.

They didn't really give her a very good reason. Mum didn't like it there anyway. She said some of the people she worked with were 'trouble' and 'not to be trusted'. She was still angry about losing her job though, especially because they made her leave behind all the inventions she'd developed there as she was escorted from the building.

Eventually, she turned her anger into science and came up with an idea that I think might be the coolest invention **EVER**.

If I tell you, will you promise not to tell anyone? I don't want to wait for your next letter to get the answer, so I'll just assume you won't tell a living soul, and if you do, something really bad will happen to you, like your **TOENAILS WILL FALL OFF**.

OK? GOOD.

My mum is working on an invention in the HSL (the garage) that can control the **WEATHER!**

Awesome, right?!

  IT'S CALLED . . .

THE WEATHER RAY!

OK . . . so it doesn't have the snazziest of names. I gave her a list of WAY cooler names, like:

- THE WEATHER-ZAPPER 3000
- THE WEATHER-BUSTER 3000
- THE WEATHER BEAM 3000
- THE WEATHER LASER 3000

(Putting *3000* after anything always makes it WAY better.)

She didn't like any of my names. She wouldn't even agree to add 3000 to her original name.

I begged and begged her to let me see it, but she said, 'Not until it's finished,' just like she always does. She *did* let me see her blueprints for it though, which I have redrawn from memory below:

You'll notice that it's not like the ray gun Zack Danger uses to zap Dr Vendetta in the last book. It's bigger and looks like a telescope, except instead of looking at the stars and the planets and all the stuff that we love doing, you have to point it at the clouds – and it can

THEM INTO WHATEVER SORT OF WEATHER YOU WANT!

COOL, HUH?

All this chemical-reaction stuff happens inside it, and then it sends your weather order into the clouds for immediate delivery!

You want five minutes of sunshine?

BEEP! IT'S YOURS!

Sick of those grey British skies?

BEEP! GONE!

Tired of walking to school in the freezing cold?

BEEP! SORTED!

Although, instead of making us have sunny skies all year, Mum wants to use it to slow global warming, which is probably a much better idea. (Not as much fun though.)

I knew having an inventor as a parent would pay off one day. Just think! When she's finished developing the **WEATHER RAY**, I'll be able to make a rain cloud appear right over Ronnie Nutbog's stupid head and pour down on him all day long. And I won't get into trouble, because my mum's a teacher! Haha! That'll teach him to mess with **THE TEACHER'S KID**.

This **WEATHER RAY** is going to change the world! There's just one problem though. Inventing weather-changing technology is seriously complicated, even for a super-nerd like Mum, so she's working every spare minute to try and develop some sort of **LIMITER** that will stop the machine from overheating and creating a crazy, out-of-control storm that could wipe out an entire town, possibly even the world . . . maybe the

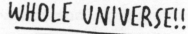

WHOLE UNIVERSE!!

I mean, that would really suck if it did happen. But Mum promised she's not even going to switch it on until she's installed that limiter, so we're **TOTALLY** safe. 'Nothing could possibly go wrong!' she says.

Anyway, write back soon, OK? I REALLY MISS YOU.
As a friend. Because you smell. Nice. You smell nice.
In a friend way. You smell like my friend and I miss
that smell.

FRANKY

PS Sorry about all that smell stuff at the end. You
don't smell. Well, you do smell a bit obviously, because
everyone smells a bit, but you don't smell bad. You just
smell of skin and hair and stuff. Which is nice. Why am
I writing about smells?! I'M SO WEIRD.

LOLZ.

BYE.

PPS Happy Valentine's Day.

MARCH

Dear Dani,

OK, don't panic, but something REALLY, REALLY, REALLY freaky has happened.

I'm not even sure where to begin. (Don't worry – everyone's still alive!)

I THINK . . .

But this is off-the-scale WEIRD.

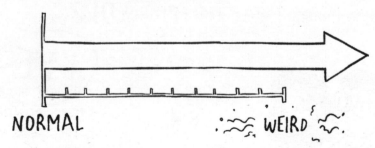

NORMAL   WEIRD

So you might want to sit down (and make sure that nosy sister of yours isn't reading this over your shoulder or I'm done for)!

It all started last night, on **PARENTS' EVENING**.

Remember how annoying parents' evening used to be – before ~~we~~ *I* came up with the **GENIUS** plan that we should **ALWAYS** blame each other when we got caught doing something cheeky?

Our super-smart blaming system meant that *your* parents thought I **WAS THE MISCHIEF-MAKER . . .**

And *my* parents thought **YOU** were . . .

FRANKY COULD DO VERY WELL IF HE PAID ATTENTION IN CLASS, BUT I THINK DANIKA CHOWDHURY IS A BAD INFLUENCE.

Of course, we didn't expect the school to make us sit on different sides of the classroom the next term, but we soon worked out our own way of communicating.

COUGH CODE:

1 COUGH = I wish we had doughnuts.

2 COUGHS = I wish we had pizza.

3 COUGHS = Possible zombie sighting in the playground!!!

4 COUGHS = Does the zombie have pizza or doughnuts?

BUT, now that MY MUM is a teacher in my new school, I don't have to worry so much about parents' evening. In fact, it's a breeze, because Mum is so busy worrying about what she's going to tell all the other parents that she couldn't care less about what the teachers say about me!

Anyway, Mum was going to be out the whole evening, so Dad was in charge of me and Max for the night.

BIG MISTAKE!

You and I both know that my dad is barely able to look after himself, let alone two children . . . especially me, and double especially MAX! As if! Like that time he took us to the ZOO . . .

But it gets worse. Because last night was also the night of the FOOTBALL FINAL! And it was Dad's team – Wigglesbottom United – versus their biggest rivals, Trumpton City.

Dad had banged on for weeks about how inconsiderate it was that the school had scheduled parents' evening on such an important night in the sporting year. 'I'm going to write a strongly worded letter to the headteacher,' he grumbled.

'If you don't stop moaning, I'll unpack the HUSBAND-O-SHHHH,' Mum warned.

Dad was quiet after that.

'That's a lesson in irony,' Mum whispered to me, smiling – but Dad's shirt still looked really creased, so I'm not sure I was paying enough attention.

YOU LIVE AND LEARN.
(That definitely felt right!)

ANYWAY, BACK TO LAST NIGHT.
PICTURE THIS:

Mum was out.

The football was on.

Dad was dressed in full Wigglesbottom kit from head to toe. You know, the one that's totally brown? Brown shirt, brown shorts, brown socks and brown shoes. Dad says they chose brown so they don't need to clean the mud off their kit in the winter. Saves a fortune on their cleaning bill, **APPARENTLY**.

And we had ordered Freaky pizza (extra cheese!) for dinner, so Dad didn't have to worry about working Mum's latest invention – the **DINNER-O-MATIC**.

We ate the pizza at the table in the kitchen while he kept running back to the living room whenever the football commentators' voices on the telly got super excited.

I don't see the point in those commentators being there. They just say the **ExACT SAME THING** you're watching.

I'm glad they don't have them on **ZOMBIE MOVIES.**

And even more relieved your nosy sister's SOPPY ROMCOMS don't have them!

. . . AND THEY'RE KISSING . . . STILL KISSING . . . STILL KISSING! I HOPE HE BRUSHED HIS TEETH!

I guessed things weren't going great with the football because Dad kept shouting things at the TV like 'FOUL!' and 'Offside!' and 'Even I could have scored that!' as well as some words that

I DEFINITELY CAN'T WRITE DOWN.

I didn't have the heart to tell him that it didn't matter how loud he shouted, the players couldn't hear him. He's thirty-four and should really know how the TV works by now.

HERE'S WHERE IT ALL STARTED TO GO WRONG.

I reached for another slice of pizza and noticed that Max had turned red. Not just a little bit red; I mean PROPER RED, like his face was going to go POP!

Since Max has only got a few teeth and can't chew his food that well, I guessed the extra-cheesy pizza was too chewy for him and that he must have a MASSIVE bit of pizza STUCK IN HIS THROAT!

There was no time to get Dad from the football and, besides, I knew from reading chapter three of the seventh Zack Danger book what to do if someone's choking. So I leaped out of my seat and ran round to

Max, ready to whack him on the back as hard as I could, to dislodge the cheesy lump he was choking on. After all, it was MY idea to order extra cheese, which meant

THIS WAS TOTALLY MY FAULT!

YOUR FAULT!!

YOU SHOULD HAVE SEEN ME RUN, DANI!

I was like a super-spy on a top-secret mission the way I leaped over the chairs and dived to save him. If it had been a movie, it definitely would have been one of those epic slow-motion shots they use in all the trailers!

I was already picturing the headlines in the newspapers:

HERO BOY SAVES BABY BROTHER!

FRANKY BROWN KNIGHTED BY THE QUEEN OF ENGLAND FOR BRAVERY

MOVIE BEING MADE BASED ON THE TRUE STORY OF FRANKY BROWN – THE BOY, THE BABY AND THE PIZZA

But, before I could save Max's life,  **THE MOST AWFUL SMELL IN THE WORLD**

shot up my nose, and I realized that the little stinker wasn't choking at all . . .

He was going red because he was **SQUEEZING OUT A POO!**

If his red face hadn't given him
away, the SMELL definitely
would have. It was beyond
yuck. It had a sharp sting to
it when it first hit my nostrils,
followed by a hint of whiffy egg
and subtle cabbage undertones.

Well, I definitely wasn't taking the responsibility
for **THAT**.

'Dad!' I shouted. 'Max needs his nappy changing!'

'The football's gone to penalties, Franky!' was Dad's
desperate reply. I could just imagine him, on his knees
in front of the TV, clutching his hair. 'I'll change him in
a minute! Just hold your nose and eat your pizza!'

I went back to finish my slice and, to my surprise,

MAX HAD GONE.

**HIS HIGHCHAIR WAS STILL THERE,
BUT IT WAS EMPTY!**

'Er, *Daaaad!*' I shouted, but he was yelling and cheering from the living room, and I guessed Wigglesbottom United had scored. I wouldn't get any sense out of him for a while.

THAT'S when I heard an almighty

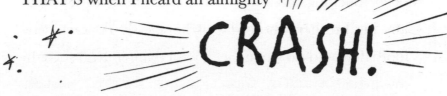

CRASH!

'Max?' I called, looking round the deserted kitchen. Where had the noise come from?

There was another SMASH!

– and then I realized: it was coming from behind the door just beside the fridge.

MUM'S HOME SCIENCE LAB!!!!
(THE GARAGE!)

I called for Dad again, and I even went to get him, but he had his face pressed against the TV screen.

Do you remember what I told you about the HSL? It's full of Mum's super-top-secret, dangerous science experiments, and we are NOT ALLOWED IN THERE. You know I am VERY respectful of rules, but I didn't have a choice. Max was in there, and he could have been touching anything – so I was about to do what any big brother whose dad is hopelessly distracted by football would do when faced with danger. Run straight towards it!

Also, I had thought of a new catchphrase I wanted to try out. It was inspired by Zack Danger because I'd just finished book twelve, *Zack Danger and the Countdown to Destruction*, that afternoon. And this was the PERFECT time to say it.

IT'S DANGER TIME!!

* I WASN'T ACTUALLY WEARING A SUPERHERO CAPE, BUT DREW IT ON BECAUSE IT LOOKS COOL!

I grabbed my pencil case from the kitchen table and snapped on my zip-that-turns-into-a-torch, aiming the beam at the door. I was ready to face whatever deadly gadgets and inventions Mum had whipped up in there.

The thing is, none of that actually happened. Before I could do that whole heroic leap thing, I spotted Max dashing across the kitchen. He can't have been in Mum's lab after all. He clambered up on to the kitchen table and, as he stood up, I saw that he was totally **NAKED!**

'Where have you put your disgusting poopy nappy?' I asked, but just at that moment, through the window behind my little brother's nuddy butt, I noticed that the sky had changed.

The clouds had got dark.

REALLY DARK.

And they were green.

REALLY DARK GREEN.

And there were little flashes of lightning.

GREEN LIGHTNING!

'Max, I think you should get down from there. I don't think we should be near the windows,' I said.

Suddenly there was a huge, deafening **BUZZING** sound that seemed to make the whole house shake.

Then

The loudest thunderclap I have **EVER** heard shook our house from top to bottom.

A **HUGE** green flash lit up the room and a gust of wind blew the kitchen windows wide open.

I jumped as my torch crackled with green light, and I rubbed my hand. It almost felt like I'd had a mini ELECTRIC SHOCK!

But there was no time to think about that now, because filling the room was a disgusting, rotten, eggy smell, like Max's poop-filled nappy but WORSE!

'Max!' I yelled. 'Get down!'

But the little naked monster just giggled and leaped on to the kitchen worktop.

I went to grab him, but I guess the fact that he had no clothes on made him more aerodynamic, because he was faster than a monkey on a motorbike and I missed him!

I chased after him, but out of the corner of my eye I saw something bad. SOMETHING VERY BAD!

Through the kitchen window, more flashes of freaky GREEN LIGHTNING were SMASHING down from the spinach-coloured sky. I saw one huge green thunderbolt zap the roof of Number 24 – Eric Flipperson's house!

Another flash of green shot down. This time it smashed into the telephone pole, electrifying the cables that ran to all the houses on our street, sending zaps of stinking green energy directly into each home. Mollie McClear, Charlie Campbell, Katy Speck, Suzy Prune, Jamelia Pointer and even Ronnie Nutbog's houses were all zapped with this strange bolt of energy from the sky, and, as the green flashes lit up their homes, I suddenly spotted their green-tinted faces peeping through their bedroom windows at this MEGA-STORM!

WEIRD, RIGHT? WELL, CHECK THIS OUT!

Next the lightning turned into hailstones the size of footballs that smashed down on to the roofs of every parked car on the street.

This was followed by MOONBEAM RAINBOWS arching across the dark green sky.

There were twisted twisters of what smelled suspiciously like BUTT-GAS . . .

YELLOW RAIN . . . not the kind you want to drink!

MUCKY MIST . . .

FLATULENT FROST . . .

HONKY HAZE . . .

The **NORTHERN LIGHTS** even showed up before realizing they were in the wrong place.

A **SANDSTORM** blew in from somewhere, then blew off again . . .

IT RAINED <u>CATS AND DOGS</u> . . .

actual cats and actual dogs!

Oh, and it SNOWED!

Then the whole house started to shake again! If I didn't know better, I'd say this was an earthquake, but that's impossible . . . RIGHT?

It was like Freaky was experiencing EVERY weather phenomenon Mother Nature can create . . .

AT THE SAME TIME!

If that wasn't strange enough, there were green flashes sparking underneath the door to Mum's lab. Suddenly the door burst open, and inside it was

CHAOS.

There was a great smouldering hole where the window had been blasted by a lightning bolt, and bubbling clouds were even forming in the lab itself. There was rain and snow and every kind of weather imaginable, all crashing around in our garage!!!

Before I could shut the door, a TORNADO of

FIZZING, SWIRLING ENERGY

escaped the lab and tore round the kitchen!

I felt my feet lifting off the floor and saw Max's nappy-less bum float past my face as he giggled.

'This is not funny!' I said. 'It's like the storm has . . .
COME INSIDE OUR HOUSE! We need to take cover!'

I had to do something. If only we had a way to change
the weather.

OF COURSE! Mum's invention – the Weather Ray!
(Or the Weather Ray 3000, as I was still calling it in my
head.) Perhaps I could power it up and zap this freaky
storm into a nice calm evening, and save Freaky from all
this freakiness.

GREAT IDEA!

I was just about to make a run for the Weather Ray
when I remembered the LIMITER – the device that

would stop the machine from overheating and creating a crazy, out-of-control storm that could wipe out an entire town, maybe the world . . . or even the universe! It hadn't been installed yet!

BAD <u>IDEA</u>!

So, instead of being a hero and saving the world, I decided to do the next best thing: **HIDE!**

I remembered that storm-chasing documentary you and me watched, when all those brave Americans with cool haircuts in awesome trucks drove into the path of twisters. Then I remembered what one of them said:

THE SAFEST PLACE IN A STORM IS UNDERGROUND!

UNDERGROUND?

Dad's man cave, in our BASEMENT!

It was every kid for himself, and I was about to run for the basement door when more headlines flashed in my mind . . .

AWESOME KID SAVES BABY FROM STINKY STORM

SUPER-BROTHER RESCUES POOPY-BROTHER

FRANKY BROWN NAMED WORLD'S GREATEST PERSON

I had to at least TRY to get Max out of there. I mean, how often do you get TWO chances to become a famous hero in one day? (Plus, it meant I could say 'IT'S DANGER TIME!' again and I was already really starting to get used to that.)

You should have seen me go, Dani. I went into slow-mo mode again, just like Zack Danger himself, only better!

SERIOUSLY!

I *think* I even did a double backflip over the kitchen table, and a wicked knee-slide under the ironing board.

I scooped up my giggling, nappy-less brother (and a slice of pizza) and made a dash for the man cave. 'Dad!' I yelled on the way, but Dad was hunched over, crying, so I guessed that Wigglesbottom United had lost and he'd probably prefer the storm to blow him away with it, so I left him there.

He was no use to us now.

After stumbling into the basement, I closed the door, leaving the freaky storm behind. Everything felt quiet and still. **WE WERE SAFE!**

Max and I made ourselves comfy on Dad's dog-chewed armchair (RIP, Billy). Max fell asleep and I found a box of Dad's Star Wars toys from when he was a kid, the ones that are still in their boxes and 'aren't to be played with'. Well, I figured it could be our last night alive – even if we did survive the Freaky storm, then Dad probably wouldn't, so I didn't have anything to lose by playing with his toys.

All the excitement of the pizza, the explosions, the funky lightning and the Star Wars figures must have exhausted me more than I'd realized. I suppose I fell asleep, as the next thing I knew I woke up in **MY OWN BED**.

That was this morning. I ran to the window and looked out at a perfectly ordinary sunrise over Freaky. Nothing had been destroyed by the green storm. In fact, it didn't even look like it had been raining! There was no damage to the cars, no damage to the rooftops of the houses I had seen zapped with lightning just a few hours before. The swing outside Jamelia's house swung gently in the breeze and Suzy's parents at Number 8 were both outside, gardening and humming to themselves.

I found Mum, Dad and Max in the kitchen. Mum was programming her breakfast order into the PANCAKE-O-MATIC.

'Morning, sweetheart! Did you have fun last night? That was a good idea of Dad's to let you sleep in his man cave away from that storm. And aren't you lucky that Dad let you play with his Star Wars toys!' Mum said, and Dad smiled at me nervously.

'Yeah . . .' I replied, relieved that Dad didn't seem mad at me (and that he had survived the storm). 'That storm was bonkers.'

Mum sighed. 'Yes, it's a shame my Weather Ray hasn't got its limiter installed yet or we could have zapped that straight into a nice clear sky in a jiffy!'

SEE, I **KNEW** THAT WOULD
HAVE BEEN A **GOOD** IDEA!

'And now you'll have to rebuild your lab too!' I said.

'Rebuild?' Mum frowned.

'Yeah, the lightning blasted a hole in the wall and there was a tornado and . . .'

Mum dropped her pancake and darted to the lab door. She ripped it open and . . .

It was totally back to normal. Spotless! Had I not seen the storm tear through the house with my own eyes, I would never have believed it.

Dad chuckled. 'You must have dreamed it!'

'As if! That's impossible!' I gasped, staring at the pristine lab.

'Nothing's impossible in there,' said Mum with a smile.

'But . . . but . . . I saw it! It was a total wreck!'

'Must have been all that extra cheese on your pizza before bed!' Mum said, shooting Dad one of *those* looks before heading into her lab to start inventing stuff.

She's still in there now and Dad's doing the washing-up. He keeps looking over his shoulder and mouthing something at me, like he's trying to tell me something without Mum hearing, but I can't quite work it out. I told him I had a letter to write to you and didn't have time to play his silly games and took my toast to my bedroom and that's where I am right now, writing this.

I guess Dad must have cleaned up the mess while I was asleep. Sometimes it's best not to ask questions. Ignorance is bliss . . . that's what Dad says anyway.

It was one **FREAKY NIGHT** in Freaky though!

Write back soon,

FRANKY

APRIL

DANI, DANI, DANI!

Thanks for your letter, it was great, but I can't talk about that now because this is an **EMERGENCY!**

This is not a drill. Something happened at school today and I don't know what to do. You're the only person in the whole ~~world~~ ~~galaxy~~ UNIVERSE that I could possibly tell because THIS IS

TOP SECRET.

Military-level top secret. If this information falls into the wrong hands, then that person's life might be in jeopardy . . .

All right, maybe that part wasn't totally true, but I just wanted to scare your nosy sister in case she WAS reading your letters. I'll assume you're alone now . . .

I CAN TRUST YOU, RIGHT?

READY?

OK.

It happened at school this morning. Every Tuesday morning, after history, we have swimming lessons in the school pool.

I can guess what you're thinking. *A school pool – your school must be one of those super-fancy posh ones with ponies and tennis courts!*

Well, think again. Everyone at my school **HATES** swimming.

First of all, the changing rooms are **FREEZING**. There are icicles hanging from the coat pegs and frost covering the locker doors. There's stinky black mould on the walls, and puddles of VERY suspicious-looking water on the floor that we try to tiptoe around.

We all have to wear these awful school-uniform swimming trunks (costumes for the girls, obviously). They're not stretchy and colourful like the kind you'd wear if you went on holiday to Barbados or Bermuda or Disneyland.

THEY'RE **REALLY GREY,**

REALLY TIGHT

AND **REALLY**

SCRATCHY.

And the worst part? Our SWIMMING TEACHER.

Mr Kovaks is nearly seven feet tall, as skinny as a goggle strap and has terrifying, pop-out, bright blue eyes like a demonic swimming robot. He is VERY CONCERNED THAT EVERYBODY LEARNS TO SWIM AND IS SAFE IN THE WATER AND THAT THERE IS NO MESSING AROUND IN HIS POOL. He shouts and screams and, whenever he shouts and screams, he also spits. (Remember those mysterious puddles I told you about?)

EVERYONE has to learn to swim. No exceptions. That's the rule.

SWIMMING
RULES

EVERYONE HAS TO
LEARN TO SWIM.

NO EXCEPTIONS.

That's totally fine by me, because I learned to swim **AGES** ago when our families both went to Funlins Family Camp for a whole summer. Do you remember? Our parents rented those awesome caravans and parked them next to each other and we had our **OWN SWIMMING POOL** in the middle, until my dad said to your dad that they should jump off the roof into the pool . . .

and then our mums made them park the caravans further away in case we tried to copy them. But it still didn't stop us trying.

Anyway, all the other kids in my class can swim too. Except for one. That unfortunate boy is called ERIC FLIPPERSON.

I think I might have mentioned Eric before. He lives on my street, like some of the other kids in my class, and sometimes we even walk home from school together. Eric's a nice kid. He's got curly blond hair and loads of freckles. He's friendly and good at art and he likes reading comics. He's pretty confident too – most of the time. But **NOT** when we have swimming lessons.

Every single time we have swimming lessons, this is what happens.

We trudge out of the changing rooms, trying to cover up our

REALLY GREY,
REALLY TIGHT,
REALLY SCRATCHY

trunks and dodging the suspicious puddles on the tiled floor. We line up alongside the pool in alphabetical order. Mr Kovaks barks commands at us, and we do some warm-up stretches. Mr Kovaks blows his whistle, and we all jump in.

The pool is even colder than the changing rooms.

Eric does not jump in. He stands by the wall. His legs go wobbly and his skin goes grey, a bit like his swimming trunks.

Mr Kovaks' pop-out eyes pop out even more.
Finally, he has to come and give Eric some
'WORDS OF ENCOURAGEMENT' to get him into the pool.

The pool isn't even that deep, and we can all touch the
bottom. I don't really see what the big deal is for Eric,
but I guess everyone's scared of something.

(EXCEPT ME! I'M NOT SCARED OF ANYTHING.)

Eric splutters to the surface, splashing and coughing
and shivering. We try to make him feel a bit better. 'You
can do it, Eric,' I whisper, giving him a thumbs-up.

'Only two lengths to go,' adds Jamelia, smiling.

That's right. The **WORST** thing about Eric not being able to swim is that the rest of us aren't allowed to get out of the **FREEZING-COLD POOL** until the **WHOLE CLASS** has completed two lengths. That means we all have to wait for poor Eric. We could whizz up and down the lanes like we were competing at the Olympics, but then we'd still have to hang about while Eric struggled and splashed.

Sometimes he actually swims (well, walks – I think his feet are touching the bottom the whole time) so slowly that it looks like he's actually going backwards and, by the time we get out, our fingers and toes are like the wrinkly elephant skin on my **GRANNY'S NECK**!!!

BUT the swimming lesson this morning was a little different . . .

We all lined up as usual, ready to jump in and get our freezing-cold lengths over and done with. Poor old Eric tippy-toed along the wall with his nervous, wobbly legs.

THEN MR KOVAKS TOOK
A DEEP BREATH.

'Today, we will be having a race!' he boomed.

'Oh no . . .' I grumbled.

'And there will be a prize for the winner!' he added.

'*Yessssss!*' I yelled.

'The person who comes first will receive this SHINY GOLD MEDAL!' Mr Kovaks said, holding up the shiniest gold medal any of us had ever seen.

Ronnie Nutbog laughed. 'I don't care about a stupid medal,' he scoffed. 'I've got loads of them at home already. Medals for swimming, medals for karate, medals for danger-skateboarding . . .'

The thing is, we all knew that Ronnie wanted that medal more than any of us. WELL, EXCEPT FOR ME!

I've never had a medal in my whole life. (I know, how crazy is that?) I wanted that medal SO BADLY that I was going to swim until my arms and legs fell off and sank to the bottom of the pool with a THUNK, and even then I'd keep swimming until I finished the race and won that medal.

I could already picture my life with it hanging round my neck, and it was a hundred per cent better than my life without it.

'On your marks, get set, go!' Mr Kovaks shouted suddenly, and we all leaped into the pool, swimming and splashing faster and harder than ever before!

I came up to snatch a breath and caught sight of Mr Kovaks giving Eric his usual 'encouragement' into the pool . . .

AND HERE'S WHERE THINGS GET FREAKY!

The exact same moment that Eric touched the water, the whole pool seemed to flash a freaky green colour. In fact, it was the EXACT same green as the lightning I saw in that storm last month.

After the green flash, a ripple shot out across the water, as though it had been zapped with some sort of energy.

It only lasted a split second. I looked around. Jamelia and Mollie and Ronnie and all the others were front-crawling as fast as their arms and legs could carry them. Everyone was so busy trying to win the race that NO ONE SEEMED TO NOTICE IT

EXCEPT ME!

Weird, right?

Well, that's **NOTHING** compared to what happened **NEXT**.

By now, everyone was at the far end of the pool, about to twist round and swim the final length. This is when we'd **USUALLY** see poor old Eric Flipperson flapping around at the opposite end as we charged back towards him . . . but not today.

ERIC WAS NOWHERE TO BE SEEN.

I felt a cold shiver down my back. If Eric was nowhere to be seen, that meant he must be

UNDER THE WATER.

'Mr Kovaks, is Eric OK?' I shouted, but my voice didn't carry over the noise of everyone splashing through the water.

Mr Kovaks stood at the side, hands on his hips, peering into the pool with a worried look on his face at the spot where Eric had plopped in. His expression turned to shock . . . then FEAR. He opened his mouth and screamed, 'SHARK!'

Everybody stopped swimming, then everybody saw it.

A long grey SHARK FIN rose out of the water and was heading STRAIGHT FOR US.

'A shark ate Eric!' yelled Charlie.

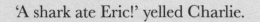

There was TOTAL PANIC!

SPLASHING!

SPLOSHING!

SPLISHING!

(Maybe even a bit of splushing . . .)

We all made a dash to get out of the pool before we joined Eric in the shark's belly, but everyone smacked and bashed into one another in the rush to climb out – and we all fell back into the water!

'I'll create a distraction!' Mr Kovaks yelled, and he ran to the side of the pool and leaped in. I thought this was pretty cool, because if I was him I would have left us all to be gobbled up – but it was no use anyway. Mr Kovaks' heroics failed when the shark used its powerful tail fin to create a

HUGE WAVE

THAT WASHED OUR SWIMMING TEACHER

STRAIGHT BACK OUT OF THE WATER!

THIS IS IT, I thought, as the shark-shaped shadow approached rapidly under the water. *I'm going to be swallowed by a shark in the school swimming pool on a cold Tuesday morning! And it was supposed to be pizza for lunch in the school canteen today too . . .*

I could picture the headline now:

Boy Genius Swallowed by Shark Moments Before Gold Medal Win

But that's not what happened. I guess you've worked that out though, because I'm not writing to you from inside a shark!

Instead of snapping me right up, the shark shot straight through my legs, totally ignoring the nice tasty children flapping about just centimetres from its razor-sharp teeth. Its smooth grey head grazed my bare toes. As it reached the end of the pool, the shark simply flipped round and swam back.

'It's . . . almost like it's trying to . . . win the race?' I stammered.

'Now's your chance! Everyone out!' screamed Mr Kovaks, and we all clambered out of the water.

I managed to heave myself out first and, as I stood up, I caught a glimpse of another green flash spreading like lightning across the surface of the water. It was followed by a grey, shark-shaped blur leaping out of the water – and

FLYING THROUGH THE AIR!

But, as the shark landed at the side of the pool, I saw that it was no longer a shark at all.

It was a small, shivering boy with curly blond hair and freckles and

REALLY GREY,

REALLY TIGHT,

REALLY SCRATCHY

SWIMMING TRUNKS.

'ERIC FLIPPERSON!' I yelled.

'Eric's alive!' Mollie shouted, and everyone ran over and crowded round him.

'Eric, how did you escape? What was it like to be swallowed by a shark?' cried a kid called Jimmy.

Eric blinked up at us and slowly shook his head.

'A shark?' he asked. 'What are you talking about?'

We all looked at one another.

'Er, there was a shark in the pool,' I told him. 'Eric, you must have seen it! It swam right past my feet!

IT <u>ATE</u> YOU UP!'

'It did not!' Eric protested. 'I didn't see a shark!'

And when we turned back to the pool . . . well, the shark had **COMPLETELY VANISHED**. It was as though it had never existed in the first place.

Mr Kovaks cleared his throat. 'Class, I think we may have all been seeing things . . . Perhaps we had, er, better not mention this to the headmaster.'

'What about the medal?!' demanded Ronnie, and everyone looked at the shiny gold medal still swinging from Mr Kovaks' hand.

'Well . . .' Mr Kovaks frowned. 'There was only one person who completed the race. So I think this medal belongs to you, Eric,' he said.

Even though I'd really, really wanted to win it myself, I was pretty happy for Eric. We all were. Everyone clapped and slapped him on the back and shouted,

'GO, ERIC!'

Eric couldn't believe it – he was gawping like a fish! And I don't blame him! Eric **FLIPPING** Flipperson, the kid who was scared of water, WON the swimming race! **CRAZY, RIGHT?**

Well, don't get too comfy. This story isn't quite over yet.

'Everyone, back to the changing rooms and get dressed,' ordered Mr Kovaks, and we all turned to leave – including Eric.

And we all saw something so weird, so strange, so FREAKY, it made Charlie gasp and Mollie shiver and all the hairs on my head stand on end.

Right in the middle of Eric's back was a

LONG SILVER SHARK FIN.

Dani, do you understand what I'm trying to tell you?

Eric Flipperson wasn't eaten by the shark.

ERIC FLIPPERSON <u>WAS</u> THE SHARK!

F-R-E-A-K-Y!

I don't know how or why it happened, but something weird made him transform the moment his skin touched the water!

ERIC + WATER = SHARK!!!

As soon as we got to the changing room, I grabbed Eric's shoulder.

'Eric,' I hissed. 'LOOK!'

He glanced in the chipped mirror and his eyes nearly popped out of his head, just like Mr Kovaks'.

We all gathered round and talked in whispers.

'What's going on?' asked Jamelia.

'I don't know, but that was the freakiest thing I've ever seen,' whispered Charlie.

'ERIC, YOU TURNED INTO A SHARK!

IT'S LIKE MAGIC!'

Eric kept staring at the fin, touching it with the tip of his finger, his face pale beneath his freckles. 'I turned into a shark . . .' was all he could say.

As we watched, his face broke into a huge smile.

'AND I WON THE RACE!' he said.

Loads of us decided to meet after school to try to work out how this had happened, so they're all coming over to my new treehouse. It's not quite finished. (There's no cinema room or planetarium just yet.) So I have to go now – but write back soon, OK?

I'm really happy that Eric finally got over his fear of swimming. Now everyone else will just have to get over their fear of swimming WITH HIM!

FRANKY

PS Do you ever get the feeling you're being watched? I do. I keep getting this weird shiver like there's someone watching me. SOMEONE IN THE SHADOWS . . .

DO YOU GET THAT? LET ME KNOW.

BYE!

Dani,

You are **NOT** going to believe this, but . . .

IT HAPPENED AGAIN!!!!!

If you thought Eric flipping Flipperson turning into a shark was freaky, then wait until you hear this.

Things have been getting weirder in Freaky, believe it or not.

Remember I told you some kids on my street were coming to my treehouse for a meeting? Well, it was pretty cramped! There was Eric Flipperson, Katy Speck, Charlie Campbell, Mollie McClear, Suzy Prune and Jamelia Pointer. And me. In fact, all the kids from my class who live on my street were there – except Ronnie **BUMFACE** Nutbog, obviously!

ERIC FLIPPERSON

KATY SPECK

CHARLIE CAMPBELL

MOLLIE McCLEAR

SUZY PRUNE

JAMELIA POINTER

RONNIE NUTBOG

We huddled inside and ran some tests on Eric.

'What sort of tests?' Eric asked nervously as I opened Mum's lab kit that I'd ~~TAKEN~~ borrowed.

'DON'T WORRY — IT WON'T HURT. TRUST ME, MY MUM'S A SCIENTIST!'

I said. 'First, we need to come up with a hypothesis.'

They all blinked at me and I suddenly knew how Miss Tinky must feel when she teaches us French.

'Hy-what-o-sis?' asked Charlie.

'A HYPOTHESIS. It's when you come up with a possible explanation for something happening, then you do experiments to test whether you're right,' I told them. 'So we need to try and think of an explanation for Eric turning into a shark this afternoon.'

'Oh right. So what's your hypo . . . hypotho . . . hypothosaurus?' asked Katy, which made everyone giggle.

IT WAS SO FUNNY!

(I GUESS YOU HAD TO BE THERE.)

'Well, have you ever been bitten by a radioactive shark?' I asked Eric.

'What? No! Of course I haven't!' said Eric.

'OK, just had to check the most obvious explanation first,' I replied.

'Hey, Franky, got any snacks? I'm starving!' Suzy asked, looking round the treehouse.

'I've got some choco-toffee-chew bars hidden under that plank of wood, and if you're thirsty there's a rainwater tap,' I said, showing them my newly installed hydration system that collects rain in a bucket on the roof and filters it into an old drinking bottle.

'WHOA! THAT'S AWESOME!' whispered Suzy.

'I guess. I learned it from watching Mum.' I shrugged. 'I haven't got the waterflow quite right yet though, so just don't unscrew it all the way or . . .'

BUT IT WAS TOO LATE!

Suzy had twisted the bottle top all the way open and a jet of water blasted across the treehouse, spraying everyone, including Eric. There was a weird flicker of green light, and . . . well, you can probably guess what happened.

And that's how we discovered that Eric Flipperson

TURNS INTO A SHARK
EVERY TIME HE GETS WET!

Luckily, because Eric wasn't totally soaked through this time – like he had been in the school pool – he wasn't a shark for very long, and after a few seconds he changed back. Plus, this time he seemed to understand what was going on a little more – so none of us got bitten. **WIN!**

Everyone helped me patch up the shark-damage in the treehouse before they went home, and we made a promise never to tell anyone what had happened there. As we climbed down the ladder, my copy of *Zack Danger and the Danger Gang* slipped out of my back pocket and landed on the grass.

'What's this?' Eric asked, picking it up.

'Oh, it's just the book I'm reading,' I said, hopping down from the rope ladder.

'That's not just a book – it's Zack Danger!' Charlie exclaimed. 'I love those books!'

I grinned. 'Me too!'

'What's so good about them?' Eric asked, so I filled them all in on how he's the coolest super-spy ever and his life is basically just one DANGEROUS MISSION.

'And in this book he has a top-secret gang of super-spies who work together to overcome any danger that comes their way,' added Charlie.

HE REALLY KNEW HIS STUFF!

Eric smirked. 'I bet this Zack Danger guy never had a mate who was a SHARK!'

Me and Charlie suddenly looked at each other for a second. I'm pretty sure we were both thinking the exact same thing and you totally would have too if you'd have been there.

'Eric's right!' I whispered excitedly as the idea was forming in my brain so fast I could hardly keep up. 'We're staring into *danger* every time we're with him, right?'

'Right,' everyone said.

'And we all just worked *together* in secret to get to the bottom of this dangerous case, right?'

'Right!' they agreed.

'DON'T YOU SEE WHAT THAT MEANS? WE ARE THE REAL DANGER GANG!'

I CHEERED.

Everyone looked at each other with excited grins on their faces. If we were in a movie, our epic theme song totally would have started to play in the background right then – as the new DANGER GANG was born!

OK, so I know I'm breaking that promise never to talk about what happened in the treehouse by writing this right now, but we both know that you'd be in the new Danger Gang too if you were here, so technically I think it's fine.

JUST DON'T TELL **ANYONE ELSE!**

We're still testing exactly how much water is needed to set Eric off, but the other day it rained at morning breaktime and before we knew it there was a shark marooned in the playground and we all had to spend the rest of break trying to dry him off with our coats and jumpers. Luckily, he'd turned back into a boy before it was time for class, so no teacher saw!

It was on that very same rainy Wednesday that the next weird thing happened. Picture this . . .

We were in maths (snore!) and Miss Tinky decided to spring a surprise test on us.

BOOM!
MATHS TEST!

The worst thing about Miss Tinky's tests are that they AREN'T WRITTEN DOWN. She makes us stand up ONE BY ONE and answer a maths question.

OUT LOUD.
IN FRONT
OF THE
WHOLE CLASS.

IT'S EMBARRASSING WITH A CAPITAL M!

It gets worse though. If you answer the question correctly, you can sit down and she moves on to the next victim. BUT, get it wrong, and you have to stay standing up and answer ANOTHER ONE . . .

. . . and, if you get that one wrong,

ANOTHER ONE . . .

. . . THEN ANOTHER . . .

. . . AND ANOTHER . . .

. . . until you finally get one right. But by that point you're red and sweaty and your legs feel wobbly like the extra cheese on a pizza.

Now luckily, having a scientist for a mum, my maths is pretty decent. I'm no Suzy Prune (she's AMAZING at maths) but I can handle myself in a surprise maths quiz and not break too much of a sweat. But there's one kid in our class who NEVER gets a SINGLE QUESTION right on these quizzes – Mollie McClear.

Mollie's one of the kids who lives on my street, at Number 19, and comes to hang out in my treehouse (and is a member of THE DANGER GANG!!! I don't think I'm ever going to get bored of saying that). Plus, we all walk to school together ever since what happened to Eric. Mollie's the quietest kid out of all of us – in fact, she's the quietest kid in class. She hardly says a thing, but always has a big smile on her face that shows off her awesome braces (she's got orange ones)!

Sometimes she's **SO** quiet, though, that it's like she's not even there at all! SHE'D MAKE A GREAT NINJA.

Ronnie Nutbog got called up to answer a maths question first. I used all my mind powers to try to push his thoughts out of his brain so he'd get the question wrong.

My powers were proved useless, though, when Miss Tinky wrote 3 X 6? on the whiteboard and I saw Ronnie fiddling around in his jacket pocket – and realized that he had his CALCULATOR hidden inside it!

Ronnie got the answer right (obviously!) and Jamelia told Miss Tinky about the calculator in his pocket, but he said that he never uses it and that's just where he always keeps it in case someone needs to borrow it!

AND MISS TINKY BELIEVED HIM!

I can't believe she falls for it, every time. Maybe her glasses aren't strong enough for her to see the

OBVIOUS FACE OF A **BIG**

STINKY LIAR!

Next up she called MY name and, when she turned round to write **8 X 4?** on the board, Ronnie threw something at me.

I caught it only to discover that it was

HIS CALCULATOR!

'Franky Brown, I will not tolerate cheating!' Miss Tinky snapped at me. She gave me another SAD FACE sticker on the chart before confiscating the calculator.

I WAS SO CROSS. I sat back down and had just started using my mind powers to make Ronnie Nutbog pee in his pants (I think I got pretty close!) when Miss Tinky called Mollie up next.

Everyone turned to look at Mollie. Some already had GIGGLE EYES, knowing that she was going to SUCK at this! Our gang tried to help her out, but there's only so much a thumbs-up across the classroom can do. She flashed everyone a brave orange-brace smile, but I saw her lip tremble a bit with nerves.

5 X 6? Miss Tinky wrote on the board.

MOLLIE WAS SILENT.

THE ROOM WAS SILENT.

Maybe even the whole of Planet Earth was silent, waiting for her to answer!

'Mollie, do you know the answer?' Miss Tinky asked. Mollie shook her head.

Then I saw Ronnie secretly holding up a little note in front of Mollie with the answer scribbled on it. I was pretty surprised. *Maybe I've got the wrong idea about Ronnie,* I thought. *Maybe he isn't that bad after all.*

Mollie glanced at it and said, 'Eight!'

The whole room cracked up laughing. Well, everyone except the kids who've been secretly meeting in my Danger Gang, obviously, because we don't laugh at each other.

WE ONLY LAUGH IN THE FACE OF dANGER.

RONNIE HAD GIVEN HER

THE WRONG ANSWER!

'Try this one,' Miss Tinky said, then wrote: 2 X 3?

Mollie thought for a while – but she simply couldn't do it. Not under the pressure of all those EYEBALLS WATCHING HER!

Then Ronnie held up another little note and made a cross over his heart to show that THIS really was the right answer . . .

'Forty!' Mollie chimed.

The other kids erupted into giggles again at another wrong answer!

I couldn't help but feel sorry for her. If I could, I would have used my mind powers to put the answer in her brain, but my two unsuccessful attempts with Ronnie had left me doubting my abilities, so I thought it was best not to meddle with her mind mid-maths test.

'Try one more. A nice easy one, Mollie,' Miss Tinky said, then wrote: 10 X 3?

Mollie was silent. She obviously wasn't born with a brain that was meant to do maths!

'Any idea?' Miss Tinky asked.

Mollie shook her head. Her smile was nowhere to be seen. From the look on her face, I could tell she was wishing she could just . . . vanish. Into thin air.

THAT WAS WHEN IT HAPPENED.

The light bulbs in the classroom suddenly flickered, then grew brighter, and BRIGHTER, and BRIGHTER, until . . .

SMASH!

They exploded in a flash of **GREEN!**

My heart skipped at the distinct and familiar colour. It was the very same green as the lightning in

THE STORM . . .

AND THE WATER IN THE POOL . . .

So I had the feeling something FREAKY might be about to happen again! My eyes darted round the room and locked with Eric's. He'd seen the flash too and I could tell he was thinking what I was thinking! I suddenly wished I'd told him my catchphrase so we could have both said it together. So I made a mental note to bring it up at the next meeting of the Danger Gang before whispering, 'IT'S DANGER TIME,' to myself.

AND I WAS RIGHT!

THEN, TO MY RIGHT, JAMELIA LET OUT

A SCREAM.

She was pointing at Mollie, who suddenly . . . didn't look right. It was hard to tell why at first. It was as if a shadow had fallen over her.

'Mollie, are you OK?' I whispered.

But Mollie just stared at us as the strange shadow grew more intense.

'No whispering during tests!' Miss Tinky croaked as she turned her back and firmly underlined the sum on the board for Mollie. It was SUPER WEIRD that she hadn't noticed the exploding light bulbs at all!

'Miss, I think Mollie might need a doctor!' said Suzy, but, by this point, it was clear that no doctor would be able to solve this problem.

It wasn't a shadow that had fallen over her, I realized. It looked more like Mollie was fading away. As though someone was using a giant eraser to RUB HER OUT!

Everyone slid off their seats and stepped away from her, except those of us who know her from the Danger Gang. We ran towards danger and tried to grab hold of our disappearing friend, but by the time we'd reached her . . .

MOLLIE McCLEAR
HAD DISAPPEARED!

BEFORE   AFTER!

We searched everywhere for her, but she was nowhere to be seen!

GONE.

VANISHED.

TOTALLY INVISIBLE!

(Just like I knew she'd wished to be.)

Miss Tinky spun round from the board, expecting to get an answer – but instead all she got was empty space where Mollie had been. She stumbled back a little in shock, her eyes searching the classroom for any sign of the vanished girl!

Just then, there was a knock at the door and our headmaster, Mr Sternly, popped his hooked nose into the classroom.

'Everything tip-top, Miss Tinky?' he honked.

'Oh, Mr Sternly, th-thank h-heavens you're here!' Miss Tinky stuttered nervously.

'My goodness, what's the matter?' Mr Sternly asked.

'It's Mollie McClear. She . . . she . . .'

'SHE WHAT?' Mr Sternly snapped.

'... SHE DISAPPEARED!'

Miss Tinky said, her face as pale as a white marshmallow.

MR STERNLY'S FACE LOOKED SO HARD IT MIGHT

CRACK
DOWN
THE
MIDDLE.

'Miss Tinky, if this is some sort of joke, then this is hardly the time. It's bad enough that Mr Kovaks thinks I'm foolish enough to believe that he needs to take a month-long holiday after seeing a shark in the school pool. A shark! Really! Of all the ridiculous nonsense. And now a *disappearing* student? Utter balderdash! What lesson are you teaching?'

'Maths,' Miss Tinky murmured, looking rather embarrassed.

'Maths, of course it is. Sounds about right. I'd bet good money that Mollie McClear is bunking class in the loo! You need to keep a closer eye on your students in the future, Miss Tinky.' And with that Mr Sternly spun on the heels of his polished shoes and marched out of our classroom, muttering something about sharks and invisible students to himself.

Before Miss Tinky had time to say anything else, the bell rang – time for our PE lesson in the sports hall – and we all left her looking under the tables for Mollie.

'What's your HYPOTAMUS?' Charlie asked as we left the classroom.

'You mean HYPOTHESIS,' I corrected him.

'That's what I said!'

'Well, I'm not sure, but I did see a green flash just before Mollie started to disappear,' I explained.

'Me too!' cried Eric.

'**SHHHH!** Not here! These conversations should be saved for the treehouse!' Suzy whispered.

'You mean **THE DANGER GANG**,' Katy added.

'The *what?*' scoffed Ronnie, who was lurking around behind us.

'None of your business and, if you hadn't been so rotten to Mollie, she might not have disappeared!' Jamelia snapped.

Mollie was so quiet before she turned invisible that I didn't think school would be all that different without her, but it turned out that, for the rest of the morning, classes without Mollie were . . . well, they were missing something.

Mollie was our fastest runner, so in PE we lost the relay race against Year Four, which was SO embarrassing.

Mollie might have been quiet, but in drama class she came to life onstage. She was supposed to be playing the lead in *Alice in Wonderland*, and today was the final dress rehearsal. Suzy had to stand in for her and she forgot all the words and ACTUALLY FELL DOWN THE RABBIT HOLE.

Mollie's dad is a pilot, so in geography Mollie always knew exactly where all the places with weird names were. She even won our class the Globe Trophy in the school competition earlier this year. On that Mollie-less day, we had to put a mark on a map of the world to show where we thought Paris was. Miss Tinky said we **COULDN'T GO TO BREAKTIME** until one of us had got it right.

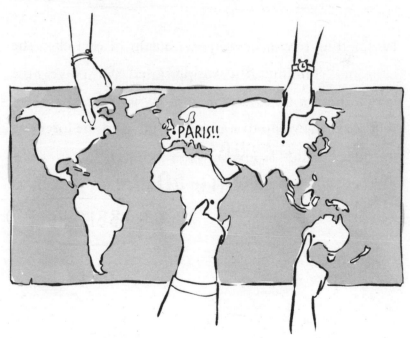

PARIS!!

WE **MISSED** BREAKTIME.

In fact, each class we had **WITHOUT** Mollie turned out to be **WAY** less fun than classes **WITH** Mollie. She might have been quiet (and **REALLY** bad at maths) but without her our class felt like the ~~Earth without the moon~~ cinema without popcorn.

AT LUNCHTIME, THINGS TOOK ANOTHER UNEXPECTED TURN.

We lined up to collect our lunch from the dinner ladies in silence. The mood was super lame as they slopped lumpy mash and mushy peas on to our plates, and we slumped into our seats at our usual table (third from the door, furthest from the water fountain . . . in case it sprays Eric) like someone had sucked all the fun out of us with a big fun-hoover.

'I MISS MOLLIE,'

huffed Jamelia, stirring her food slowly.

'ME TOO,'

agreed Eric, taking a gulp of his lunch.

'ME THREE,'

I added, not feeling hungry.

Then, out of the blue, Ronnie Nutbog – who was sitting at the table next to ours – sighed. 'Yeah,' he said. 'I thought school was rubbish anyway, but I guess it's even more rubbish without her smiling orange braces to brighten the day.'

We all fell silent and stared at him. It was the first time anyone had ever heard him saying something nice about anyone.

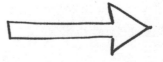

All of a sudden, a huge green splodge of mushy peas flew across the table and landed with a

SPLAT!

on Ronnie Nutbog's face!

Ronnie scrambled to his feet straight away. 'Whoever threw that is DEAD MEAT!' he yelled, glaring around at everyone.

We looked at one another. But none of us saw who threw it. It was almost as though it had been thrown by someone INVISIBLE!

SPLAT!

A second dollop of peas sploshed over Ronnie's clothes.

'AHHHH!' Suzy screamed, pointing her finger at something by the water fountain. We all turned and saw

THE FREAKIEST THING . . .

A hand, floating in mid-air. It was only visible because it was dripping with mushy peas!

'That can only belong to one person,' Eric whispered.

I nodded. 'Mollie! She must have been here the whole time!'

But there was no time to think about that now. The hovering hand plunged into a pile of lumpy mashed potato and flung another splodge across the table, showering ALL OF US with sloppy mash!

That's when I had my brilliant idea. I got to my feet, took a deep breath and yelled: 'FOOD FIGHT!'

Total chaos broke out. Hot dogs flew like javelins across the canteen! Burgers became frisbees! Baked beans poured like raindrops from the sky, as the ENTIRE school got stuck in!

I managed to land a direct hit with a carrot stick in Ronnie's ear, but he saw me throw it and aimed his next round of sausage-roll ammo at me (which really hurt)!

By the time Miss Tinky came bursting into the canteen, it was a total wreck. We were all covered head to toe – even Mollie McClear, who looked like some sort of food-monster!

WAIT — MOLLIE WAS BACK!

'MOLLIE, YOU'RE BACK!'

we cheered as she wiped away the sloppy food and we saw her as clear as day again!

'I've been here the whole time. You just couldn't see me! I heard the nice things you said about me when you thought I wasn't there,' she said, grinning. 'Thanks.'

Suzy cleared her throat and said, 'You're sorry for making fun of Mollie being rubbish at maths. Aren't you, Ronnie?' She nudged him in the ribs.

'Yeah, 'spose so. Everyone's rubbish at something. I guess your thing is maths,' he mumbled, not taking his eyes off the food-covered floor.

'That's the thing!' Mollie said. 'I'm actually GREAT at maths!'

Well, we were all super confused when she blurted that out.

'So why do you always get the answers wrong?' I asked.

'I just get so nervous standing up in front of everyone that my mind sort of goes blank, and the answers won't come out of my mouth!' Mollie explained. 'When everyone's staring at me, it's like you're all waiting for me to get it wrong, so it just sort of happens! It's not like in drama where I can pretend to be someone else.'

We looked at each other. Suddenly I was feeling SUPER guilty that, in a weird way, we were the reason Mollie was so bad at something she's actually good at!

'Sorry, Mollie,' I said.

'Yeah, sorry,' added Charlie, and Katy and Jamelia nodded.

'It's OK,' she replied, shrugging. 'It's amazing what you see and hear when you're invisible. I think maths tests might be a bit different from now on.' She winked.

We were all sent to the changing rooms to wash off the mess in the showers (which made Eric transform into a shark again).

When we got back to our classroom, Miss Tinky asked us to sit down. Then she said, 'Would whoever started the food fight in the canteen please stand up.'

THE ROOM WAS
DEAD SILENT.

Only our eyes dared move as we looked round to see if Mollie was going to own up to starting the (best) food fight (ever).

Out of the corner of my eye, I saw her slide her chair back and start to stand when . . .

'IT WAS ME, MISS,' SAID RONNIE NUTBOG!

'I'm very disappointed in you, Ronnie,' sighed Miss Tinky as she placed a SAD FACE sticker next to Ronnie's name on the chart, before sending him off to help clean up the canteen as punishment.

As he left, he turned round and gave Mollie McClear a little wink – which might just be the freakiest thing I've seen in Freaky so far!

We all turned and looked at Mollie, who was grinning from ear to ear, more visible than ever before.

'As for the rest of you, for taking part in the food fight you'll have to suffer ANOTHER maths test to make up for the one we had to cut short this morning!' Miss Tinky trilled, expecting the usual groan of despair from us all. But instead she was greeted with a cheer. Not only could we SEE Mollie again, we were going to SEE her maths skills in action.

'Very well,' Miss Tinky scoffed, picking up her thick glasses that were hanging on a cord around her neck. 'Mollie McClear? I'm glad you have reappeared from wherever you "vanished" to this morning,' she said, removing her glasses to check her eyes weren't deceiving her. 'Well, now that you are here, you can go first! What is 8×7?'

TOUGH ONE! I thought.

There was a tense silence as we all swivelled round and gave our now-very-visible Danger Gang friend a secret thumbs-up. This time, we weren't expecting her to get the answer wrong.

AND SHE DIDN'T!

So I have a **SHARK-KID AND AN INVISIBLE GIRL** in my class. What will happen next?!

Write back soon,

FRANKY

PS Remember I told you before that I felt I was being watched? Well, I thought I just saw a dark shadow in the front garden when I came home from school today, like someone walked across the grass, but there was no one there. **MUST HAVE IMAGINED IT, RIGHT?**

JUNE

Dear Dani,

I wish you could see the Danger Gang headquarters (my treehouse)! It's looking cooler than ever. We all meet there once a week after school, to eat sweets, practise saying,

'IT'S DANGER TIME!'

(OK, that's mostly me) and discuss any crazy new things that have happened . . . and yes, **MORE** things have happened since my last letter!

Charlie's mum works at the newsagent's at the end of my street, right next to the pet shop, and she lets Charlie have whatever he wants so he always stops by the shop before our meetings and grabs **LOADS** of top snackage to keep our brains fuelled for our chats. (Four choco-toffee-chews and a tub of nutter-crunch ice cream for me every time.)

THREE KEY THINGS
HAVE HAPPENED SINCE MY LAST LETTER:

FIRST, Mollie has learned to control when she disappears and reappears. She worked out that she can do it whenever she wants just by doing this weird little twitch with her nose. I'M BEYOND JEALOUS!

SECOND, to balance out that awesome discovery, here's some significantly less awesome news. Ronnie Nutbog, AKA BUMFACE, now comes to our weekly meetings.

I KNOW!

Since the food fight and him being nice to Mollie, the gang took a vote and everyone else decided to give him a chance. So I had no choice . . . plus, I suppose that is the right thing to do. But I've told him that he's one wrong move away from being booted out of the treehouse and have since added EJECTOR SEAT to the top of the list of things to install when I eventually get to phase two of the build.

THIRD, I went to my FIRST PARTY here in Freaky.

AND IT WAS A NIGHT
                I WILL NEVER FORGET.

It was Charlie Campbell's party. He lives on my street too, at Number 16, and he's a member of the Danger Gang! He's also crazy about dangerous animals. It's all he blabs on about.

'When I'm older, I want a pet cobra!' he says . . .
EVERY DAY!

'Aren't they poisonous?' asks Katy . . .
EVERY DAY!

'You mean *venomous!*' he corrects her . . .
EVERY DAY!

Suzy said he's been into 'weird' and 'dangerous' animals for as long as she's known him, and those two were born in Freaky, so I guess that's a pretty long time.

On the night of his birthday, his mum and dad were taking us all to the fairground in the park, and after that we were going to his place for a sleepover.

I was **SO** looking forward to going. You know how much I love sleepovers. Remember that time I slept at your house and we ordered pizza and they accidentally delivered TWO PIZZAS instead of one? That might still be the best night of my life.

I LOVE PIZZA . . .

Where was I?

OH, AT THE FAIRGROUND! It was only stopping in Freaky for one night so EVERYONE in town was there. By the time we arrived, the sun was setting, all the neon lights were on and the air smelled so good I

could have had it for dinner. Actually, I did have it for dinner! We ate candyfloss, roasted caramel nuts, triple-fudge doughnuts, hot dogs, lollipops, and I had a toffee apple just to make sure I got one of my five a day.

Everyone wanted to go on the Ghost Train, but I said I'd already been on the Ghost Train last year when the fair came to my old town and it would just be **BORING** to ride it again.

But Ronnie Nutbog said I was just scared and that I would probably **PEE MY PANTS** with fright on the ride. So I went on it to prove I wasn't afraid.

I DIDN'T PEE MY PANTS...

I did spill my slushy on my trousers though, so it **LOOKED** like I did. But I **DIDN'T**! I wasn't even scared. You know how brave I am!

SLUSH AND
NOT PEE!

I dried off my **SLUSHY-WET** trousers by riding the teacups and Ronnie Nutbog spun us round so fast it made Jamelia puke.

Mr and Mrs Campbell said we needed to calm down before we went back to Charlie's house, so they bought us all freshly popped sweet 'n' salty popcorn out of one of those big machines that smell awesome, and we all went on the Ferris wheel – which turned out to be pretty cool because you could see our houses from the top!

On the way to his house, Charlie revealed loads of **BIG** plans for his sleepover.

'I'm going to ask Mollie to turn invisible, then she can secretly throw a cup of water on Eric to transform him into a shark, and we can see if he can use his heightened shark senses to track her down,' he whispered excitedly to me.

My heart sank. **THAT SOUNDED SO EPIC.** I mean, it's not very often that you get to have a sleepover with an invisible friend and a shark!

But my inner super-spy instincts knew that I had to make his dreams vanish quicker than Mollie in a maths test, and when we got to Charlie's house I broke the news that the sleepover was to remain a

SHARK-FREE ZONE.

'Why?!' he asked.

'Eric turning into a shark, Mollie turning invisible . . .
We have to keep these things **TOP SECRET!**
You of all people should know that. What's Zack
Danger's number-one rule about secrets?' I asked,
knowing full well that any true Zack Danger fan would
know this.

**'SECRETS AREN'T SECRET IF YOU DON'T KEEP
THEM SECRET,'** he sighed, quoting *Zack Danger and the
Secret Traitor* word for word.

'Exactly. We need to keep this information to ourselves,
just the Danger Gang, so no liquids are to be consumed
around Eric tonight, and Mollie needs to promise to
stay visible the whole time!' I said.

As if my new rules for Charlie's sleepover weren't bad
enough, the moment we stepped into Charlie's house,
Mr and Mrs Campbell handed out a sheet of their own

'SLEEPOVER RULES' that they'd even had laminated in plastic to make them indestructible, which is a terrible way to start any party.

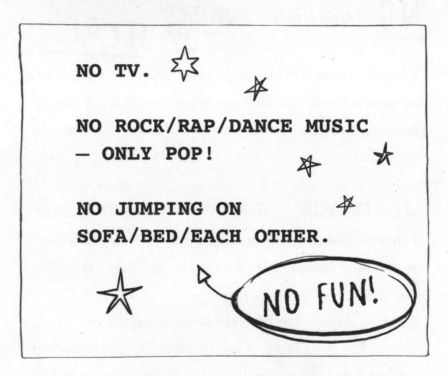

NO TV.

NO ROCK/RAP/DANCE MUSIC — ONLY POP!

NO JUMPING ON SOFA/BED/EACH OTHER.

NO FUN!

Someone should tell grown-ups that decorating rules with glittery stars doesn't make them any less lame. Once Mr and Mrs Campbell had disappeared into the kitchen, I quickly scribbled my own Danger Gang rules at the bottom . . .

NO DRINKING WATER AROUND ERIC
NO TURNING INVISIBLE

. . . and explained the whole *secrets aren't secret unless we keep them secret* thing, and we all made a Danger Gang promise.

So a few minutes later there we were, sitting on Charlie's living-room floor, playing pass the parcel like a bunch of five-year-olds, listening to music by some ancient band that the grown-ups seemed to like that I'd never heard of.

There was a huge sigh of relief when Charlie's dad said,

'PRESENT TIME!'

Now here's the thing. Remember I told you that Charlie is ANIMAL MAD? Well, for almost as long as the Danger Gang has existed, Charlie has been banging on about how he's going to get a PET for his birthday. But he doesn't know what sort of animal it is.
It's a surprise! So we've all been guessing.

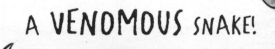

A VENOMOUS SNAKE!

A SCARY ROTTWEILER

A MONKEY

A BIRD-EATING
SPIDER

AN ALLIGATOR

TWO ALLIGATORS!

OK, so some of our guesses were a bit out there, but it was Charlie and he was obsessed with those kinds of bitey, stingy, deadly animals. So it was pretty exciting waiting to see which super-awesome animal Charlie was going to be calling his pet as we gathered round to watch him open his presents.

The first boxes contained the usual stuff: pyjamas, a new lunchbox. To be honest, it was a total snorefest until his dad brought out the **FINAL PRESENT**.

I don't know why parents always leave the best present until last. When did they all get together to decide to do this?

It's like leaving your favourite bit of dinner until the end. By the time you get to it, you're so full up of presents that you can't eat any more.

WAIT . . .
WHY AM I TALKING ABOUT EATING PRESENTS?

You know what I mean.

Anyway, Charlie's dad carried his last present out in a special box with **HOLES** in the top, and we all knew that could only mean **ONE** thing:

THERE WAS SOMETHING **ALIVE** INSIDE!

Charlie tore open the box with an enormous smile on his face.

Was it a deadly venomous snake? The world's most stingy jellyfish? A baby alligator that he could train to bite his enemies in the playground?

Charlie reached inside, and we all stepped back as he pulled out . . . the fluffiest furball any of us had ever seen!

A HAMSTER!

WHAT A LET-DOWN!

All those precious minutes we'd spent imagining our friend owning some sort of awesome creature from the jungle or the depths of a swamp, and it turned out to be a ball of fur from Freaky Pets – the pet shop at the end of our road.

On the other hand, it was at least four times fluffier than a regular hamster – and it had bright green eyes.

'What kind of hamster is it, Mr Campbell? I've never seen one like this!' asked Katy, who **KNEW LOADS** about hamsters because she has two of her own.

HAMSTER EXPERT

'Well, the man at the pet store wasn't quite sure himself. You see, these hamsters just appeared in his shop the other month, as if by magic! He had no clue where they came from,' Mr Campbell explained.

'What, you mean he didn't know one of his hamsters was pregnant and had hamster babies in the night?' Katy asked.

'No! It's the strangest story. He told me that he'd sold ALL his hamsters that day and the cages were empty when he locked up in the evening. There was a big lightning storm later so he came in early to check on the animals, and when he opened up he found a cage full of these fluffy little things!'

Well, I bet you're thinking that my heart pounded in my chest when he mentioned the lightning storm – and you're right. It was going boom! BOOM! BOOM! And as I looked around at my friends I could tell their hearts were boom! BOOM! **BOOMING** TOO!

Could the hamsters have appeared because of **THAT STORM?**

'What are you going to call him?' Mrs Campbell trilled.

Charlie didn't know. I think he had loads of ideas for Rottweilers and snakes and bird-eating spiders, but not so many for fluffy hamsters.

'I have an idea! Let's each write a name on a piece of paper and fold it in half. Then we'll put our hamster names into a bowl, and Charlie, you can pick one out at random,' suggested Mrs Campbell, rushing to get some paper and pens.

We all scribbled down our ideas and dropped them into the bowl.

'My hamster will officially be known as . . .' Charlie said as he plunged his hand into the bowl – and, would you believe it, he pulled out the name **I HAD WRITTEN!**

'GANGSTA
THE HAMSTA!'

Charlie announced.

Everyone laughed and said what a cool name Gangsta was for a hamsta . . . everyone except the grown-ups.

'Gangsta isn't a real name, Charlie. You'll have to choose a different name from the bowl,' Mr party-pooping Campbell said.

So Charlie chose again, which was totally out of order if you ask me.

'My hamster's new name is . . . MR FLUFFLES,' Charlie read out, and this time his parents looked relieved.

'Mr Fluffles isn't a *real* name either!' I argued.

'Charlie can call his hamster whatever he likes,' Mrs Campbell said.

'Except Gangsta?' I replied, and she gave me a look that seemed to have the same effect as Mum's KID-SHUTTER-UPPER.

Charlie let Mr Fluffles run around on the floor for a bit and we all watched. He was cute, but pretty boring. Mr Fluffles didn't really *do* anything, so Ronnie flicked a piece of leftover popcorn from the fairground towards him, and we watched the hamster store it in his cheek pouch.

THAT WAS ABOUT AS EXCITING AS MR FLUFFLES GOT.

Charlie sighed with disappointment at not getting something remotely wild or dangerous. I guess Mr Campbell realized, as he scooped up Mr Fluffles and put him back in his cage to take up to Charlie's bedroom. 'As it's a special day,' he announced before he left, 'you can stay up until *midnight*.'

I don't know if they were letting us stay up late to make up for getting Charlie a hamster instead of an alligator, but it made us all really excited, because everyone knows that the best things happen at midnight! Plus, I'd been starting to worry that Mr and Mrs Campbell might be PARENT-BOTS set to BORING MODE and that Charlie was in need of rescuing from a life of laminated rules and awful pet names, so I could at least put that out of my mind now.

BORING MODE!

At about eleven o'clock, us boys got into our sleeping bags in Charlie's living room (the girls were sleeping upstairs in Charlie's bedroom).

Mr and Mrs Campbell checked on us one last time.

'Remember, lights out when the big clock dongs midnight,' Mr Campbell said, pointing to the grandfather clock standing in the corner of the room, and we all nodded politely before they went up to bed.

The moment we heard their bedroom door shut, we pulled out the snacks we'd secretly stuffed in the bottom of our sleeping bags.

I CAN'T BELIEVE PARENTS DON'T KNOW ABOUT THAT TRICK YET! (HAHA!)

I'd brought the classic jumbo pack of marshmallows and a slightly squished but delicious choco-glazed doughnut. Eric had jelly babies, and Ronnie had steak-flavoured crisps (weird choice!). But then Charlie laughed at us as he unlocked and opened a door just off his living room to reveal a cupboard FULL OF SWEETS!

'IT'S BEAUTIFUL,' whispered Eric.

'IT'S AMAZING!' I added.

'MIGSH MAWHSHODDOM,' mumbled Ronnie through a mouthful of crisps.

'It's all the stock for Mum's shop!' Charlie grinned.

'You stole the key?' Eric gasped.

'Don't be daft! She always lets me have the key on my birthday! Dig in!'

With that, he dived into this sugary cave of wonders.

We were all whispering, until Charlie told us that his dad snores so loudly that his mum has to sleep with earplugs in, so we could make as much noise as we liked and they'd never wake up!

Mr and Mrs Campbell were quickly becoming the **COOLEST PARENTS EVER!**

We chatted and laughed as we shared out handfuls of jelly beans and Smarties and crisps and . . .

MIDNIGHT!

It had sneaked up on us like a wizard wearing an invisibility cloak and, from the corner of the room, the old grandfather clock was chiming its order to go to bed.

But, with no chance of waking up Mr and Mrs Campbell, we just ignored the chimes of the clock.

UNTIL . . .

'Shhhhh!' Ronnie hushed us. 'Do you hear that?'

We all listened. As the clock dinged its last dong, the bells turned into . . . SCREAMS.

'It's the girls! Upstairs!' Eric gasped.

HE WAS RIGHT. THEY WERE SCREAMING!

Me, Charlie, Ronnie and Eric legged it up the stairs as fast as we could, ready to be the heroes that saved the sleepover!

FRANKY BROWN SAVES SLEEPOVER

But, the moment we crashed through Charlie's bedroom door, we skidded to a stop at the sight in front of us.

I knew something freaky was happening because the whole room was glowing green. The very same eerie glow as the lightning in the storm, the water in the pool and the light bulbs during the maths test – but this time it was coming from

THE HAMSTER CAGE!

'Something weird is happening to Mr Fluffles. I've not read about this in ANY of my hamster books!' screamed Katy, looking at the hamster, who was glowing a luminous green.

I took a step closer to the cage and stared at something I will never be able to unsee. Gangsta (aka Mr Fluffles) wasn't just glowing.

He was GROWING!

His fluffy body was stretching and expanding in the light of the midnight moon.

His spiky fluff was poking through the bars of the cage, making the metal bend and creak.

'He's going to break out!' I cried, but it was too late.

The first bars went PING!

and TWANG! across the room as

MR FLUFFLES BURST OUT OF HIS CAGE.

He stood fully upright on his back legs and stretched to the sky, glowing a vibrant pukey green like some sort of furry Hamster-Hulk monster!

'Now **THAT'S** a cool pet!' Charlie cheered.

But, at the sound of Charlie's voice, the humongous, human-sized hamster turned its glowing green eyes on US!

Now I realize I'm the bravest person you know, but even I was scared when Mr Fluffles leaped across the room! I swear, for a second, I thought he was going to eat me, or at least store me in one of his cheek pouches!

But he went straight past me and stuffed his fluffy, oversized nose into a half-eaten bag of popcorn from the fairground!

'He must be hungry!' Charlie realized. 'Quick, hand over your snacks!'

The other boys and I fished around in our pockets and the girls dug into their sleeping bags to reveal their sleepover snacks too. We handed them all to Charlie to give to Mr Fluffles. I was gutted that I'd run upstairs with my choco-glazed doughnut and now had to hand it over to Charlie to feed to his hamster!

'Don't do it, Charlie!' Jamelia shrieked. 'He'll eat you alive!'

'I've got to. If he doesn't eat this, he might eat *us*!' Charlie said.

Of course, I would have stepped up and fed the creature too, but I have a baby brother at home to be a role model to. If something happened to me, I couldn't bear to think about what Max might end up like, so I did the brave thing and let Charlie feed the ravenous, TWO-METRE-HIGH RODENT ALONE!

'He's only eating the popcorn! And he's eaten it all!' Charlie hissed in a nervous, high-pitched whisper. The fluffy monster then started leaping round the room, scratching at the windows.

'He needs exercise!' Katy the hamster expert spluttered. 'The popcorn's given him lots of energy, and he'll have to burn it off! That's why hamsters have wheels in their cages!'

'That's great, Katy, but how do you plan on exercising a GINORMOUS HAMSTER?!' snapped a trembling Ronnie from behind the bed. 'I mean, it's not like there's a giant wheel for him to run on!'

When he said that, an idea popped into my head as though that invisible wizard had whispered it in my ear.

'THAT'S IT!' I CRIED.

'What's it?' Charlie asked.

'A giant wheel!' I said, pointing out of the bedroom window where, over the rooftops, in the distance, we could see the twinkling lights of the fairground, still lit up against the night sky. Towering above it all was the

FERRIS WHEEL!

'A giant wheel!' I whooped. 'Plus, that place has loads of popcorn that he can eat. It'll be empty now too, so no one will see Mr Fluffles!'

Without hesitation, Charlie went into full Indiana Jones mode and whipped the belt out of a dressing gown hanging on his bedroom door. He lassoed it round Mr Fluffles and leaped on to the giant hamster's back! I guess reading all those books on dangerous animals paid off!

'To the fairground!' he commanded, and the mutant rodent seemed to understand his words. It was as though Charlie had some sort of special ability to communicate with his pet. They charged out of the bedroom, down the stairs and burst through the front door.

We all armed ourselves with torches and followed them out into the night, hopped on anything with wheels that was lying around Charlie's garden and chased after them!

It turns out it's not hard to follow a giant rodent being ridden by a child, as they were setting off nearly every car alarm as they tore through the streets of Freaky. We rode our bikes past car after car with smashed mirrors, broken headlights, shattered windows.

'I told you Charlie should have called him Gangsta,' I called to the others as we looked at the trail of destruction.

We arrived at the deserted fairground to find Charlie and Mr Fluffles at the enormous Ferris wheel. The giant hamster leaped straight to the top and began sprinting as fast as he could, with his tongue flapping happily out of his mouth!

'I KNEW THIS WOULD WORK!'

cheered Charlie, watching his monstrous new pet, beaming with pride.

He ran faster and faster, just like hamsters do on their little wheels in their little cages – except this one was

MASSIVE! Suddenly sparks started

fizzing from the enormous hamster wheel. And not just
any sparks . . . **GREEN SPARKS!**

'Er, Charlie . . . I think something's happening!' I said.
'Look – those sparks aren't coming from the wheel.
They're coming from Mr Fluffles!'

The sparks didn't slow him down though.

HE GOT FASTER . . .

AND FASTER . . .

AND FASTER . . .

UNTIL . . .

A cloud of green smoke puffed into the air where Mr Fluffles had been running and, when it cleared, the huge hamster had vanished.

'He's gone!' we all gasped as Charlie leaped towards the giant wheel. He crouched down, his head hanging low, looking sad.

'What's wrong?' Katy asked.

'Where's Mr Fluffles?' Jamelia choked.

'Is he . . .' I couldn't finish the question.

Suddenly the silence was broken by a tiny little SQUEAK!

'You're alive! You're alive!' Charlie cheered. He scooped up the now perfectly unharmed, hamster-sized Mr Fluffles and gave him a huge fluffy cuddle. 'I thought I'd lost you for a second!'

WE ALL CHEERED.
HE WAS ALIVE!

And the risk of being MUNCHED by a ginormous hamster had gone!

Then we headed back to Charlie's house as the sun was starting to rise, and by the time we got there it was morning. As the front door closed behind us, Mr and Mrs Campbell were coming down the stairs.

'Blimey, you're awake early! Have you been outside?' Mr Campbell asked.

We looked nervously at each other. I mean, we could hardly say, *Yes, we went back to the fairground to let the mutant hamster you bought your son have a run on the Ferris wheel so he wouldn't eat us!*

Charlie said, 'Yeah, Katy said hamsters like exercise so we let Mr Fluffles have a run around on the grass in the front garden.'

Mr and Mrs Campbell looked at each other.

'Charlie, that's very responsible!' Mr Campbell beamed. 'If you keep on looking after Mr Fluffles like this, perhaps you could have one of those more wild and exotic pets for your next birthday.'

Charlie held up Mr Fluffles and looked into his deep green eyes.

'You know what, Dad? I've changed my mind. I think maybe this little hamster is wild enough for me.' Charlie grinned and we all burst out laughing.

Needless to say, it was
THE **BEST** SLEEPOVER EVER!

Wish you could have been there, Dani!

FRANKY

PS I've just remembered! When we were at the fairground, I'm 89.9 per cent sure that I spotted that shadow again. The one I saw move in the front garden.

CAN SHADOWS FOLLOW YOU? **WEIRD!**

JULY

Dear Dani,

HAPPY BIRTHDAY!

How was your party? The photos you sent in your letter looked great. Who was the boy sitting next to you? The one that looked like this:

I don't recognize him. Is he a new kid? How old is he? Are you friends? What did *he* get you for your birthday? I bet it wasn't half as good as my present. It's an ACTUAL fossil of <u>ACTUAL</u> DINOSAUR POOP! How ~~gross~~ *awesome* is that! <u>HAHA!</u>

I knew you'd love it. Mum helped me buy it for you, except she wanted me to get you one of those boring swirly fossils – you know, the ones that look like snails? But I knew you'd prefer some prehistoric <u>BUM ROCKS</u>.

Anyway, back to me.

I'M ON <u>SUMMER HOLIDAY</u> NOW!

But I HAVE to tell you about something that happened in the last week of school before we broke up.

As our end-of-term treat, Miss Tinky took us on a school trip to the Freaky Falls waterpark.

Freaky Falls is **AWESOME**! It's got all these waterslides that go upside down and twist round and round. There's even one called **TIDAL FORCE** that does a LOOP-THE-LOOP. Ronnie said that **EVERYONE** pukes at the end . . .

. . . but that turned out to be a load of **RONNIE RUBBISH**, as usual.

Still, it was going to be an awesome school trip because ANY school trip is awesome as there are:

(A.) NO LESSONS,

(2.) NO LESSONS AND

(D.) NO LESSONS!!!

We were all **SUPER** excited about it.

Well, everyone except Katy Speck.

'I HATE Freaky Falls!' Katy huffed in the classroom as we waited for the coach to show up.

'Why?' I asked.

As soon as I said it, I realized I already knew why, and I wished I could take it back.

'I'm TOO SMALL!' Katy whined. She jumped down out of her chair and stood up as tall as she could. Her head only just made it to the middle of my chest.

Katy lives on my street too, at Number 23, and she's part of the Danger Gang. She does gymnastics and guess what? She can do an actual backflip! It's super awesome! I told her Zack Danger can do backflips, and since she'd never read Zack Danger before I lent her the first book and she's reading it at the moment.

She's also the smallest of all of us. In fact, she's the smallest kid in class by a long shot.

'I went to Freaky Falls last year with my mum, and the only slides I was tall enough to go on were the baby ones in the kids' pool,' Katy said sulkily.

'Well, that was a year ago. You've probably grown since then!' I said encouragingly – but deep down I was thinking,

THERE'S NO WAY YOU'RE TALL ENOUGH FOR THE PUKE-LOOP SLIDE.

'Don't worry, Katy. If you can't go on the waterslides, you can sit with me in the picnic area. I can't get in the water . . . obviously! We'll have fun in the sunshine and fresh air instead!' said Eric.

But, as we walked across the car park to the coach, there was a buzzing, whirring sound in the air around us, and I suddenly stopped mid-step. I was remembering something from that morning, as Mum had waved me off to my classroom. She'd shouted something at me and now I had the feeling it was going to be important.

Trouble is, I hadn't totally been listening. I was thinking about Zack Danger trapped in the shark-infested waters of Count Malvo's lair in chapter twelve of book seven, and wondering how he was going to get out of this one (and thinking I should definitely lend that book to Eric when I was finished with it).

'Have a great time at Freaky Falls!'

She definitely said that.

'We've won the lottery and you won't be coming back to school tomorrow – we're moving to a mansion in Hawaii!'

Pretty sure she didn't say that . . . So what was it?

AND THEN I HAD IT.

'Franky, watch out for flying ants today!'

'GUYS, IT'S FLYING ANT DAY!'
I YELLED.

Whoever invented flying ants is a right twerp. I hope it wasn't my mum.

Ants are rubbish at the best of times. If you ever leave a sandwich on the floor for a split second, you can bet there'll be an ant in it when you take a bite. I mean, who even cares if they can lift up really big leaves? That's only useful if you're an ant and, as I've already established, **ANTS ARE RUBBISH!**

There's only one way I could possibly think of making ants even more annoying than they already are, and that's giving them wings, and **THEN** giving them one day every year when they **ALL** come out to have a great big **STUPID** Flying Ant Party where they fly in your face and in your can of fizzy drink and up your nose and in your toilet and in your bowl of Honey Hoops and on your pencil when you're writing the answer to a test so you get it wrong. Basically:

FLYING ANTS
ARE TOTAL RUBBISH

AND

EVEN MORE RUBBISH

THAN NORMAL,
NON-FLYING
ANTS.

When it comes to bugs, they are off the bottom of the chart.

BUG AWESOMENESS CHART
(FROM COOL TO LAME)

10. BEE – *because they make honey and Honey Hoops is the* **BEST BREAKFAST CEREAL EVER** *and we wouldn't have it without bees.*

9. PRAYING MANTIS – *those things look like ninja-robots!*

8. DRAGONFLY – *awesome name! Would be even better if it was Dragonfly 3000 though!*

7. SPIDER – *especially radioactive ones that give superpowers.*

6. BUTTERFLY – *anything that can transform from a gross little worm-with-legs into a colourful flying creature definitely deserves to be number 6.*

5. CRICKET – *because in Zack Danger and the Desert of Doom he survived for two weeks just by eating crickets!*

4. BEETLE – *because there's that one that rolls giant balls of dung . . . and dung is poop . . . and poop is funny.*

3. WORM – *yeah, worms are pretty lame. Taste gross too. But they're not as lame as a . . .*

2. MOSQUITO – *so annoying!*

1. WASP – *evil.*

0. ANT – *just why? What's the point?*

-1. FLYING ANT!

I'm assuming they don't need to pass any sort of flying test before they're given these wings either, because half of them don't know which way is up and which way is MY FACE!

If you don't know what Flying Ant Day is, I'll tell you. It's the day when all the girl ants and all the boy ants come out of their little ant houses to MAKE ANT BABIES —

I know, right? It's even worse than you first thought.

As we hopped on to the coach, I swear the buzzing sound got EVEN LOUDER. I guess the ants were singing ant love songs to each other.

I told Miss Tinky that the school should make Flying Ant Day a school holiday so we can all just stay at home and pretend it isn't happening, but she just told me to sit down while the coach was moving.

So there we were, stuck outside in our swimming costumes in the flying-ant-filled 'fresh air' ALL DAY. Every time you came up for breath, you were guaranteed to get a flying ant in the mouth.

It really seemed to suck all traces of adventure out of us. Even Ronnie wasn't in the mood to muck about, and just wanted to get this trip

OVER AND DONE WITH!

We just about survived the morning. By lunchtime, Jamelia had multiple red patches on her face from where she'd tried to swat away flying ants and missed, and I'd swallowed about seven of them.

MISSED!

The only time we got a break from the flapping of little ant wings was when we were whizzing through the tubes of the waterslides, surrounded by a force field of plastic! But poor Katy was still too short to be allowed on them, and had to wait at the bottom, watching us through a cloud of ants.

Katy watched us ride AQUASPLASH.

'I'm sorry, you're not quite big enough for this one yet, little girl,' said the Freaky Falls ride operator when Katy tried to get on with us.

She watched us ride H2-WHOA.

'Oops, maybe next year, kiddo!' said another.

She watched us ride **WILD WAVE 3000** (great name!).

'This one's for BIG kids,' another told her.

She watched us ride **SURF-STORM**.

'Have you lost your mummy?' another asked her.

She even had to watch us slide down **TIDAL FORCE**, the ride with the loops. And, I'm sorry to say it, but it was as awesome as I'd hoped.

'There's the Lazy Stream over in Funderland, our special area for our youngest visitors,' suggested another ride operator. 'It's slow and safe for little ones like you.'

After that, Katy sighed and gave up trying to get on the waterslides with us. She trudged towards Funderland and the Lazy Stream, which looked like it was made for *really* little kids to go on with their mummies and daddies.

'Excuse me, Katy,' called Miss Tinky. 'The class needs to stay together. You can't go on waterslides on your own, thank you very much.'

'But . . .'

'No buts!' she insisted.

We all saw the look on Katy's flying-ant-covered face as she slumped back to watch us all have fun on another awesome waterslide.

That's when I came up with a plan.

'It's OK, Miss Tinky. We were all about to go and ride on the Lazy Stream – WEREN'T WE?' I hinted, shooting a look at the others.

'No way!' barked Ronnie, missing the point as usual.

'Yes, we were!' insisted Suzy, nodding at me.

'Isn't the Lazy Stream a bit small and slow for you lot?' asked Miss Tinky, eyeing up the

SLOWEST RIDE IN FREAKY FALLS!

'Nah, the slower the scarier!' I lied.

'The Lazy Stream seems brilliant!' added Mollie.

Miss Tinky looked puzzled, but shook her head. 'Very well then, off you go. Be back in an hour, please. Katy, your friends are coming with you.'

'Thanks, guys. You really don't have to though,' Katy said, her face red with embarrassment as we wandered into Funderland. The place was **PACKED** with three-year-olds and their parents, splashing in the little fountains of water that spouted up through the non-slip padded floor. It was armband central and we were the oldest kids there by a long shot!

'Right, what shall we go on?' Jamelia said, looking around at the selection of awful attractions, such as . . .

- **SLIPPY-SLOW-SLIDE** . . . which was definitely slow, but not very slippy.

- **SHALLOW SHOWERS** . . . where a plastic elephant sprayed a gentle mist from its trunk every few minutes.

- And, of course, **THE LAZY STREAM** . . . that gently trickled its way round the whole of Freaky Falls. It was no deeper than your average puddle and you had to sit in these lame inflatable rings. *SNORE!*

KIDS AREA

But the most BORING attraction of ALL was **MINI-FREAKY FALLS** – which was just a replica of Freaky Falls, but really, REALLY small and all you could do was look at it. You had to watch tiny little model people bob up and down in tiny little model pools and slide their way down the waterslides before being dragged up on a mini conveyor belt to slide down them again.

I mean, what grown-up in their right mind thought it would be remotely interesting to build everything just **REALLY SMALL?**

'Well, I guess we start on the Lazy Stream,' Jamelia said, trying to sound a little excited for Katy.

'Yeah . . . I guess,' she said with a sigh.

As we approached the ride, a Freaky Falls employee dressed as a mermaid appeared, wearing a wiry green wig and a big green foam mermaid-tail. She smiled at us before closing the gate to the ride and hanging a sign on it that said:

LAZY STREAM TEMPORARILY CLOSED!

'Sorry, kids. This ride got struck by lightning a few months ago and it's been flowing faster and faster every day since. We've had a few complaints from parents today, so maintenance are on the way to slow it down. We'll have it up and running again for your next visit,' the mermaid said, giving us a cheery swish of her tail.

My heart did a loop-the-loop in my chest.

228

THANK GOODNESS IT'S CLOSED!

I thought to myself – but I thought too soon!

'Oh, but PLEASE, can't you let us on? Just us . . . for ONE lap round the stream?' begged Mollie.

I tried my best to catch everyone's eye, to warn them that we didn't want to go on this ride after all – but they were too busy trying to convince the mermaid to notice.

'This is our friend, Katy, and she's too small to ride any of the fast slides,' added Jamelia.

Ronnie shoved Katy in front of the Freaky Falls mermaid and Katy did her best sad face, which was really convincing because she was actually gutted about this whole situation.

The mermaid sighed and looked over her shoulder to see if anyone was looking.

'OK, OK,' she said. 'But just one lap, then I've got to close it, OK?'

Everyone cheered (everyone except ME!) and ran past the mermaid and into the Lazy Stream, which was definitely the worst water ride I'd ever been on.

Obviously, everything in my brain was telling me *not* to go on this ride. I mean, I now **KNEW** that this ride had been struck by lightning in the storm. That was the storm that had led to Charlie's freaky hamster being born! And the more I'd been thinking about it, the more I was convinced it was that storm that had given Mollie and Eric their crazy abilities too!

I just had a feeling that going on this ride could only lead to ... **WELL, <u>SOMETHING</u> YOU'RE ABOUT TO FIND OUT ABOUT!**

So there we were, sitting in inflatable doughnuts and floating along, with Eric waving us off.

'See you downstream!' sang the mermaid as the water carried us away . . . **SOOOO** . . . **SLOWLY!**

'This is rubbish!' grunted Ronnie, splashing his fist in the water, forgetting how shallow it was and punching the floor.

'No it isn't. I like it!' said Mollie loyally, glancing at Katy.

Katy shrugged. 'It's OK. Ronnie's right. This *is* super lame. I'm sorry you all had to come on here with me. Being small sucks!'

WE WERE QUIET FOR A MOMENT. Suddenly Charlie flung his arms up in the air and started screaming as though he was riding the fastest waterslide in the whole of Freaky Falls.

Everyone cracked up laughing and joined in, and before we knew it we were swaying left and right in unison round imaginary bends, holding our breath as we dived

→

through invisible waterfalls, and screaming with fear over stomach-churning drops that didn't exist.

As we splashed and swayed, I couldn't help but notice that the water was beginning to change colour. What was once a pale blue stream was turning a **LITTLE GREENER** with every splash of our imaginary water ride, until we were all floating through flowing, luminous green water!

Katy hadn't noticed. **SHE WAS LAUGHING SO HARD SHE COULD HARDLY BREATHE!**

'That was the **BEST RIDE EVER**!' she cheered as we splashed into the exit. 'I guess being small isn't all that bad if you have a big imagination!'

We climbed out of our doughnuts and on to the bank of the stream and shouted, 'Thanks!' to the mermaid as we went through the exit.

But the mermaid didn't reply.

'We said THANK YOU!' repeated Katy.

Again, the mermaid said nothing. Not only that, she was perfectly still, in exactly the same position she'd been in when we got on the ride.

OK, Dani, here's where things get really freaky, and I just want to prepare you so you don't scream!

HERE WE GO THEN . . .

We walked over to the mermaid to check that she was OK, but as we got closer we could see that something wasn't quite right. Something had changed about her.

Her wiry green wig wasn't wiry any more. It looked like it was made of solid plastic. And it wasn't just her hair that looked like this. So did her swishy foam tail . . .

AND HER FACE . . .

AND HER HANDS . . .

'Are you OK?' asked Katy, stepping a little closer to her and reaching out her dripping wet hand. But, as she touched the mermaid's shoulder, her body toppled forward and she fell face first to the ground with a loud

SMACK!

Everyone gasped as we all saw that the mermaid was now made entirely of PLASTIC!

REAL MERMAID!

'What's going on?' Ronnie asked, looking alarmed.

'I'm not sure . . .' replied Suzy. 'But whatever happened to the mermaid must have happened to them too.' She pointed at the crowd of young kids with their parents, who had been splashing around Funderland, and who were now frozen like plastic models.

Suddenly the ground started shaking.

'EARTHQUAKE!' Charlie screamed.

BOOM!
BOOM!
BOOM!

An enormous face appeared in the sky above us.

'I don't think that was an earthquake!' I said to Charlie. 'It was a GIANT! RUN!'

We ran for cover as the enormous person towered over us, then an EVEN BIGGER GIANT appeared next to the first one and pointed down at us.

'You see, son. It's a model of Freaky Falls!' he said, smiling.

'What's the point of that?' the kid-giant scoffed before running away, causing the ground to shake around us.

We all stared at each other for a moment, trying to take in the words that we had just heard.

'Guys, I don't think we're in Freaky Falls any more . . .' I said, staring out into the perfect replica of the waterpark that we were now standing in. 'We're in MINI-Freaky Falls!'

THAT'S RIGHT, DANI — WE HAD SHRUNK!

Something had happened to us when we went on that Lazy Stream, and we were now standing INSIDE the model.

I knew as soon as I'd heard the words 'struck by lightning' that I should have shouted '*It's Danger Time!*' and we would all have just run away as fast as we could!

'HELP!' Ronnie started screaming.
'SOMEBODY HELP US!'

'I don't think they can hear you,' Suzy said, as we watched the little kids – who were now ENORMOUS little kids – sploshing around the full-sized park in the distance.

Suddenly there was a great crash of water behind us and we whipped round to see the model of . . .

'TIDAL FORCE!' said Katy in delight.

It was right there in front of us. An exact replica of that amazing waterslide.

'Let's go!' Katy cried as she ran over to the entrance. There was a model of the ride operator, and Katy stood next to the model of the height indicator.

'Well, technically, I'm still too small to go on this,' she said.

'But it's not like he's going to stop you, is it?' grinned Ronnie, waving his hand in front of the ride operator's frozen plastic face.

'Let's ride!' I shouted.

And, with that, we all leaped on TIDAL FORCE, racing our way to the top of the tower and diving into the tubes of rapidly flowing water.

After that it was AQUASPLASH,

followed by H2-WHOA,

straight on to WILD WAVE 3000,

then SURF-STORM!

'That was AMAZING!' screamed Katy at the top of her tiny lungs at the end of every waterslide. 'This is the BEST. SCHOOL TRIP. EVER!'

But, just then, we heard a strange sound, carried on a gust of wind that swirled our dripping wet hair over our faces as we looked around, trying to work out where it was coming from. It was a deep, deafening noise from overhead, like army helicopters coming in to land. Except **THIS** wasn't army helicopters . . .

Remember what day it was, Dani? That's right!

'IT'S A SWARM OF GIANT FLYING ANTS!'
I yelled.

'Whoa!' we all cried. The wind from their powerful wings beat down on us as they performed a fly-by of the model waterpark we were standing in, like fighter planes at an air show!

'I think they're coming back!' screamed Katy, pointing to the sky as the flying ants wheeled round. They dived down low and weaved in and out of the fake buildings before landing in the middle of the Funderland section to take a drink from the shallow pools of water.

'GET LOST! GET LOST!'

screamed Ronnie, as he shooed away these horse-sized ants.

'Awesome!' whispered Charlie. 'Wild ants!'

'*Flying* ants!' added Katy.

'Are you thinking what I'm thinking?' asked Charlie, staring with wonder at the giant insects.

With the power of hindsight, I can safely say that none of us were thinking what Katy and Charlie were thinking, as you will now see from what they did next.

They ran straight towards the largest of the group of ants and **LEAPED ON TO ITS BACK!**

'First it's giant hamsters, now it's giant ants!' yelled Charlie.

'FLYING ANTS!' cried Katy, as the ant spread its wings and shot into the sky.

We watched and our jaws hit the floor.

'Well, I guess we'd better go after them!' Mollie said.

A few nervous minutes later, we were all sitting on our own flying ant, and together we shot into the air, WHOOSHING faster than any waterslide in Freaky Falls. The ants zoomed us around in perfect formation, just like the RED ARROWS!

'Look, there's Katy and Charlie!' Ronnie shouted, spotting our friends in the distance as they dive-bombed

the ride operator who hadn't let Katy ride TIDAL FORCE.

We caught up with them and raced our flying ants round Freaky Falls, weaving in and out of people's heads, diving low under dripping wet feet. Katy even managed to reach out and scoop a handful of Eric's ice cream as she whizzed past the picnic area.

'I love being small!' she cried through a mouthful of vanilla ice cream, and we all replied with a cheer. Being small was **AWESOME!**

Then, as we soared high over the waterpark, we saw the coach that was to take us back to school pull up outside – and Miss Tinky searching for us!

'How are we going to grow up?' called Ronnie from his flying ant.

'You could try tucking your shirt in and washing regularly?' replied Mollie.

'No, I mean grow **BIG!**' shouted Ronnie. 'We can't stay small forever!'

I already knew the answer to that. This whole thing had started with lightning magic, and it could only be

ENDED WITH LIGHTNING MAGIC.

'Follow me!' I called over the buzzing of my ant's wings as I dived back towards the model waterpark.

We landed our flying ants in the middle of miniature Funderland and I led everyone back on to the Lazy Stream for one final ride.

We climbed into the doughnuts and began our second voyage round the world's slowest water ride – complete with green sparks and flickers as we bobbed along the lightning-struck stream.

As we floated into the exit, the mermaid was standing on the bank, waiting for us, her wiry wig blowing in the breeze.

'WELCOME BACK TO FUNDERLAND!'
she chirped.

We leaped out of the stream and ran back into a busy, full-sized world. We had made it out alive and were normal size again – just in time for Miss Tinky to come marching into Funderland, looking for us.

'Where have you been? I said ONE HOUR. I've been looking for you everywhere!' she snapped.

'Sorry, Miss Tinky – we had a LITTLE adventure!' Katy grinned and we all cracked up.

'Well, the coach is here and you all need to dry off and get changed!' she said, ushering us towards the changing rooms.

And that was the end of

THE **BEST** SCHOOL TRIP EVER

and why Flying Ant Day now might be my favourite day of the year!

WRITE BACK SOON!

FRANKY

PS Shadow update: spotted at Freaky Falls, outside the gift shop to **TIDAL FORCE**. I lost sight of it when a big family walked past, but it looked like this . . .

It's the shadow of a person, right? Except there was **NO ONE** AROUND.

AUGUST

Dear Dani,

Summer holidays are well and truly underway in Freaky. The weather has been hot, the sun has been very sunny and I have to say ... I'M KIND OF MISSING SCHOOL!

WAIT,
DID I ACTUALLY
JUST WRITE THAT?

I'm going to have a lie-down for a moment. I'll carry on writing once I've confirmed that my mind hasn't been taken over by one of Mum's inventions designed to turn me into a super-nerd.

I'M BACK and I can't find any evidence of my mind having been tampered with, so I guess I genuinely do miss school a little bit. If you tell anyone I said that, I swear I'll tell your sister about that time you used her super-expensive shampoo and panicked because you thought she'd notice that the bottle was half empty, so you refilled it with another bottle you found in the bathroom cupboard that *looked* similar but turned out to be **BLUE HAIR DYE!**

Her hair was blue all summer and she never did find out why! I know I shouldn't laugh but . . .

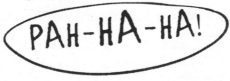

PAH-HA-HA!

Like I was saying, it's **HOT** in Freaky! There's a hosepipe ban because it hasn't rained for three weeks, so Eric is safely in human mode at the moment. I haven't seen Mollie much since school finished, but I think that's because she went on holiday to France with her mum and dad for a few weeks, rather than she'd turned invisible. She did get back a couple of days ago though, so I guess she could be standing next to me, reading over my shoulder **RIGHT NOW**, and I would never know . . . or right next to **YOU** for that matter!

Every night, I see Charlie sneak out of his back door with a bag of sweet 'n' salty hamster-transforming popcorn in his hands and Mr Fluffles, the **GIANT** hamster, on a lead. (Yes, through our treehouse investigations we learned that it's **SWEET 'N' SALTY POPCORN** that makes Mr Fluffles change from regular furball to

HAMSTER-HULK! Sweet or salty on their own just make him do eye-watering hamster bum-trumps.) They go for a walk up and down our street. I know this because Mr Fluffles leaves a trail of . . . well, you know what **(POOP!)**, and you **DO NOT** want to step in that stuff.

So my summer holiday has been pretty 'normal' compared to all the stuff that's happened since moving to Freaky. I've had absolutely nothing to write to you about . . .

I was coming home from the shop (I went out to get an ice cream . . . yes, it was a nutter-crunch, STILL my favourite!) when I spotted Ronnie crouched behind Eric's wall with a bucket of water balloons.

Now this wasn't a surprise. Ronnie has been camped out like this most days since the start of the summer holidays, waiting for the perfect moment to lob a balloon at Eric and turn him into a SHARK.

That's no surprise either. No matter how many times we see Eric transforming, it NEVER gets boring. Plus, Ronnie loves a good prank. I mean, who doesn't?

DING!

That gave me an idea.

A bad idea.

A **GREAT** IDEA!

With Ronnie's attention focused on Eric's window, it would be *sooooo* easy to sneak up on him, slip a water balloon out of his bucket and **SPLAT** it right on *his* head.

Oh, that would be *sooooo* satisfying. He would **NEVER** see it coming!

But you can't do that, Franky, I thought to myself.

Yes, you can! said another little voice in my head.

You can't! Ronnie would bosh you on the nose. Yes, he's a tiny bit less of a pain in the bum than he used to be, but he's still Ronnie Nutbog! said the first voice – the sensible voice!

But only if he caught you. (The second voice had a good point.)

What if I did it and ran away super fast? You know that I'm a good runner, and don't even think about saying that you're faster, Dani. You beat me **ONCE** and I had a verruca that really slowed me down!

VERRUCA

Well, no prizes for guessing which voice I listened to.

I AM A MEMBER OF THE
DANGER GANG AFTER ALL.

I gulped down the last of my nutter-crunch, tippy-toed up to the closest tree and peered round at my target, who was still hiding behind the wall, looking at Eric's window.

IT WAS _TOO_ EASY!

I crept over as quiet as Zack Danger on a super-secret spy mission and slipped a big water balloon out of the top of Ronnie's bucket. It felt heavy in my hands and, as it glistened in the sunshine, I thought I saw a mysterious green shimmer across its surface, like it was full of magic ready to burst.

I took aim and **LAUNCHED** it at the back of Ronnie's shaved head!

SPLAT!!!

DIRECT HIT! The balloon burst and released what looked like an ocean of freezing water all over his head!

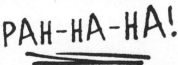

PAH-HA-HA!

In all the excitement, I nearly forgot to RUN AWAY!

I quickly turned and started to leg it as fast as I could, back to my hiding place behind the nearest tree. My heart was pounding so hard I could see my T-shirt jumping up and down!

When I peeked round the trunk, I saw Ronnie wiping the water from his face and looking around for whoever threw the balloon. After a few seconds, he shrugged, crouched back down by his bucket and continued to wait for Eric.

HA, THAT GOT HIM! I thought to myself, and I was about to go home when something caught my eye.

The front door of Number 23 was opening just a creak. Katy peered through it, then shot outside in a flash with a great big mischievous grin on her face.

I stayed hidden and watched her sneak up behind Ronnie, just as I had done. Slowly and quietly, she pinched a water balloon from his bucket, took aim and sploshed it right over his head.

HA! She must have seen me do it and thought it was a **GREAT IDEA!**

Katy might be small, but all that gymnastics practice means she can move really **FAST!** She leaped back over her garden wall and ducked down flat before Ronnie could dry his eyes.

'Whoever did that is **DEAD MEAT!**' he growled.

Well, I was about to go home AGAIN when I heard another SPLASH!

I turned to see what looked like Suzy dive into a bush, and Ronnie covered in ANOTHER of his exploded balloons.

Next came Charlie . . .

SPLASH!

Even sweet little Mollie popped out for a throw. She was invisible, of course, so Ronnie had NO CHANCE of seeing her coming!

SPLASH!

Then Jamelia took aim too!

SPLASH!

IT WAS A TOTAL WIPEOUT.

SPLASH!
SPLAT!
SPLOSH!

We all giggled from our hiding spots as a dripping wet Ronnie lay defeated on the ground.

THAT'S WHEN IT HAPPENED . . .

the freakiest thing I've seen since moving to this town (and you know that's saying a lot!).

Ronnie Nutbog started <u>**CRYING**</u>.

I mean, forget sharks in the school pool and giant hamsters. THIS WAS TRULY BIZARRE!

We all emerged from our hiding places and glanced at one another.

I didn't know what to do. None of us did. Ronnie was the toughest kid in the whole school. None of us had ever seen him CRY before!

One by one we slowly went over to him.

'Sorry, mate, it was just a joke,' I said, giving him a little nudge – but he carried on sobbing.

'Yeah, we didn't mean it,' added Katy, biting her lip.

'You do stuff like that to us all the time, Ronnie. We just thought we'd give you a taste of your own medicine!' said Charlie, but that just made Ronnie cry

EVEN LOUDER!

'Shhhhh!' said Jamelia, looking around. 'If a grown-up hears you crying, then we're all in deep doo-doo!'

We all thought it at the same time. Getting us in trouble was **EXACTLY** what Ronnie was trying to do! There was no way he was really crying over a little bit of water on the hottest day of the year.

Looking at the soaked grass was like looking at a crime scene. The victim – Ronnie Nutbog – lay in the middle. Around him were six guilty assailants . . . Katy, Suzy, Charlie, Mollie, Jamelia and **ME!**

'I'm not pretending! They HURT!' Ronnie wailed dramatically – but I was watching him closely, and made out a tiny glimmer of a smile.

THE CHEEKY SO-AND-SO
WAS PRETENDING!

But the more he pretended to cry, the more the tears became real tears. You know that feeling when you pretend something so hard that it becomes real? **THAT** was what Ronnie was doing!

'Keep it down or we'll all be grounded for this!' I hissed.

'Stop being a **BABY!**' Suzy snapped.

Ronnie stopped crying suddenly.

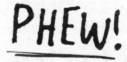

'What did you call me?' he said, sniffing.

'A baby!' Suzy huffed. 'Because you *are* a great big baby!'

Ronnie just stared at her, and he didn't look too great. His freckly face had gone very pale, like he was going to be sick or something.

'Ronnie, are you OK?' I asked.

But, instead of answering me with words, Ronnie looked me in the eyes and said, 'GOOGOO-GAGA!' in the most convincing **BABY VOICE** I'd ever heard.

Then Katy let out a scream. We all gasped and took a hasty step back, because what happened next was truly crazy!

RONNIE WAS SHRINKING!

I don't mean like when we all shrank to the size of ANTS last month at Freaky Falls. Ronnie wasn't just getting smaller . . .

HE WAS GETTING *YOUNGER* TOO!

Right in front of our eyes, Ronnie Nutbog went from **KID** to **BABY** in about ten seconds flat, until all that was left of him was a wriggling little Baby Ronnie in a pile of Big Ronnie's clothes.

NATURALLY, WE <u>RAN AWAY</u> SCREAMING.

Then Baby Ronnie did what all babies do: he started to cry! This wasn't like Big Ronnie *pretend*-crying; this was actual, EAR-PIERCING BABY-CRYING – and that's something that grown-ups simply cannot ignore (no matter how much they wish they could)!

One by one, we all crept back and circled the screaming baby.

'Charlie, pick it up!' said Suzy.

'No way! *You* pick it up!' he replied.

'No chance! I've never held a baby before in my life!' Suzy snapped.

'Neither have I!' confessed Jamelia.

'Me neither,' added Katy and Mollie.

THEN ALL THEIR EYES TURNED TO <u>ME</u>.

I was about to tell them that I hadn't held a baby before either, but they knew about Max, so there was **NO** chance I was getting away with it!

'All right, all right, I'll pick him up!' I said as I bent down and carefully scooped up little Baby Ronnie, being careful to support his head like Mum had drilled into me when Max was born, and wrapping him in his own T-shirt, which was now **MASSIVE** on him.

'Now what?' I asked, looking down at the little human in my arms.

'Let's just take him to his house, ring the doorbell, leave him on the doorstep and pretend nothing happened!' said Suzy.

'We can't just *leave him on the doorstep*! His mum and dad will never believe it's him!' I said.

'Let's take him to the police – they'll know what to do,' said Charlie.

'Hang on a second. Eric turned into a shark, but he turned back into a boy again. Mollie, you turned invisible and you reappeared eventually. Charlie, even Mr Fluffles shrank back to his usual size. And we all grew back to normal size on Flying Ant Day! Ronnie will change back too. We just have to give him time to . . . grow up!' I said.

'First, I think it might be time to change his nappy,' said Suzy, holding her nose.

'ER . . . HE'S **NOT WEARING** A NAPPY!' I said.

As soon as Suzy spoke, the smell of Baby Ronnie's poop seemed to fill the entire street.

WE ALL GAGGED AND HEAVED.

'He can use one of Max's nappies. Let's get him to my house, quick!' I choked.

We ran back to mine and sneaked in through the back door and into the kitchen, hoping Mum and Dad wouldn't notice . . .

'What have you got there then, son?' Dad said.

'Oh, we're just playing a game, Mr Franky's Dad,' Katy lied, while I tried to keep Baby Ronnie hidden.

'Yeah, er, we're playing . . . um, babies,' added Charlie.

Dad stared at us. He must have suspected something.

THIS WAS IT.
WE'D BEEN CAUGHT!

'Off you trot then, but keep the noise down. Your brother's having his nap,' he chimed with a wink, and we all rushed upstairs.

We crept silently into Max's room, found his nappies and laid Baby Ronnie on the changing mat.

'Go ahead,' I whispered, handing the wipes to Suzy.

'Me? Haha! Not a chance!' she hissed, shoving the wipes back into my hands. 'You started this – you can finish it!'

I couldn't argue with that. I *did* throw the first balloon.

'OK, here goes nothing,' I said before taking a deep breath and . . .

WIPING RONNIE NUTBOG'S POOPY BUM!!!!

IT WAS THE GROSSEST THING I HAVE EVER, EVER, **EVER** DONE!

Thankfully, having a baby brother has given me some experience in the nappy-changing department and I managed to get it done with minimal mess, and also without throwing up everywhere (Jamelia looked like she was pretty close).

I threw Ronnie's poop-covered T-shirt away, dressed him in some of Max's baby clothes and we crept back downstairs. When we arrived in the kitchen, Ronnie started to cry again! (Luckily, Dad had wandered off into the living room.)

'NOW what's wrong with him?' asked Charlie.

'I think he's *hungry*!' I replied.

'Here . . . these are his favourite,' said Suzy, offering me a chocolate bar she had stuffed in her pocket.

'He's a baby! He can't have that!' I replied.

'It's *Ronnie* – he **LOVES** chocolate,' Mollie said. But there was no way I was going to feed a choco-toffee-chew bar to a toothless, nappy-wearing baby. Instead I grabbed one of my brother's bottles, filled it with warm milk and started to feed Baby Ronnie.

THIS IS SO WEIRD.

YOU WEREN'T THE ONE WIPING HIS . . .

'Still playing babies?' chirped Dad, wandering back into the kitchen and still completely failing to notice that we had a real baby with us.

'Yeah, feeding time now!' Mollie said.

'Oh yes, of course! Don't forget to burp him after,' Dad said, playing along, and not realizing he'd actually totally reminded me that we needed to do that!

'Nice one, Dad! We're going to take him for a walk,' I said, and we all headed out of the front door as Dad chuckled to himself.

SOMETIMES IT REALLY DOES PAY OFF HAVING A COMPLETELY CLUELESS DAD.

We walked down the street towards the spot where Big Ronnie had become Baby Ronnie, and all gathered round to take a look at him.

'Aw, he's actually pretty cute now that he's not covered in you-know-what. Can I hold him?' asked Mollie.

'Sure! You can burp him if you like!' I said, and carefully handed him over.

As Baby Ronnie stared at us with his big blue eyes, we forgot for a moment that *this* was the kid that gave us MEGA-WEDGIES every morning before assembly or dished out random dead-arms on the way home – even since we'd all become sort-of friends with him. I had to agree with Mollie that somehow this baby version of Ronnie *was* kind of cute!

Baby Ronnie belched a deep, slightly green, gassy burp as Mollie rubbed his back.

'Blimey, that was a good one!' I said. 'Try again!' Mollie gave him a little pat on the back and . . .

BUUUUUURP!

Another impressive, deep burp was released, but something else had happened too . . .

'Does Baby Ronnie look a little bigger to you?' asked Suzy.

We all had a closer look and agreed that Baby Ronnie had grown.

'Burp him some more!' Jamelia said, and Mollie started patting him again.

BUUUUUUURRRRRP!

He grew . . .

BUUUUUUUUUURRRRRRRP!

He grew some more . . . and he wasn't just growing bigger. He was GROWING UP!

'More!' we all cried, and Mollie patted the toddler's back.

BURP . . .

'MORE!'

BUUUURRP!

'MORE!'

BUUUUUURRRRP!

'MORE! MORE! MORE!'

BURP! BUUUURRP!
BUUUUUUUUUURRRRRRRP!

By this point, Mollie had to lower him on to the grass, because he was almost as big as her – and he was nearly back to his real age. Just one more burp would do it! Mollie swung her arm and gave him a great big wallop – but, instead of just burping, Ronnie did something I've seen my baby brother do a hundred times . . .

RONNIE NUTBOG THREW UP ALL OVER US!

We were covered, head to toe, in warm milk, fresh out of Ronnie's belly.

SO GROSS!

By the time we'd wiped it out of our eyes, we were face to face with a rather confused-looking, regular Ronnie.

HE WAS BACK!

'What's going on, and why am I wearing baby clothes?' he asked, blinking at us, but just as I was about to open my mouth to try to explain, I spotted something flying through the air towards us.

IT WAS A WATER BALLOON!

'Yes!' cheered Eric from his bathroom window. 'Gotcha! I've been waiting to do that ALL week!'

We couldn't tell if it was water or tears in Ronnie's eyes, but none of us were sticking around to find out.

Well, that's been the freakiest part of my summer so far and if I learned anything from that day it's *never* to call Ronnie Nutbog a **BABY**. (It's a pretty good idea not to call anyone names, full stop, I reckon.) And I've got a feeling Ronnie might just have learned a lesson too. In fact, he's been *almost* nice to us ever since. Hardly any wedgies at all!

Who'd have thought we'd be learning so much in the summer holidays?

HOPE YOU'RE HAVING A GREAT TIME!

FRANKY

PS With all this summery sunshine, I thought I'd definitely spot the shadow again, but nothing yet. HOWEVER, after Eric soaked Ronnie and I ran back to my house, I couldn't help but notice that there was an **EXTRA** set of wet footprints on the dry pavement . . .

SEPTEMBER

Dear Dani,

SUMMER IS WELL AND TRULY <u>OVER!</u>

The first day back at school was grey and rainy and just a little bit too cold, but everyone had **NEW PENCIL CASES!** Which **TOTALLY** made up for everything because nothing is better than a <u>**NEW PENCIL CASE!**</u>

Suzy had a flappy plastic one, Mollie had one that you could see through, and Eric had a shiny metal one that was indestructible (unless Ronnie Nutbog stamped on it).

Technically, I didn't have a **NEW** pencil case. I still had the awesome one that Mum made for me when we first moved to Freaky. But it was still the coolest of everyone's! I got it out and showed off the secret compartments and detachable yoghurt spoon and mega-bright torch, which to be honest hasn't totally been the same since the night of the storm, but still works just fine as long as you don't mind a little electric shock every now and then. Which is lucky for me, because without it I'd be in a whole heap of doo-doo right now, and here's why.

Once the initial pencil-case excitement wore off and learning began, things quickly settled into the usual lesson vibe. But then Miss Tinky went and made this month **TEN TIMES** better by dropping some awesome news.

'Class,' she announced, 'some of you may already know that in a few days' time there's going to be a very special event above our town. **A TOTAL SOLAR ECLIPSE.**'

Everyone thought this was super **AWESOME**, but not because of the rare astronomical phenomenon that would align the sun, the moon and the Earth so perfectly that the moon would cause a total **BLACKOUT** in the **MIDDLE OF THE DAY** . . . No, the kids thought this was awesome because . . .

$\Longrightarrow$

'And, so that we can observe this phenomenon, you will all be having the afternoon off school,' added Miss Tinky.

THAT'S RIGHT!
WE WOULD ALL BE GETTING THE AFTERNOON OFF SCHOOL!

But, to my left, I noticed a shaky hand being raised in the air.

'Yes, Jamelia?' asked Miss Tinky.

Jamelia looked terrified. 'Miss,' she asked,

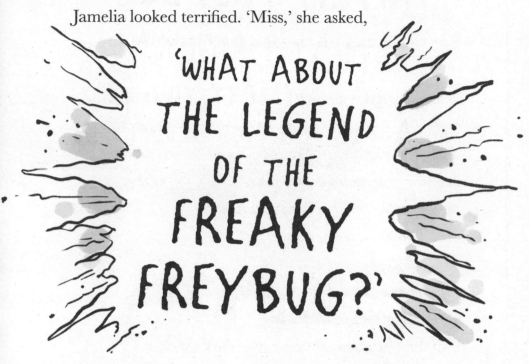

'WHAT ABOUT THE LEGEND OF THE FREAKY FREYBUG?'

No, I had no idea what a FREYBUG was either.

Some of the other kids in my class knew what Jamelia was talking about, but most didn't, so Miss Tinky wrote this ancient poem about it on the board. It was pretty cool already, but I've spiced it up a little to make it even better . . .

THE LEGEND OF THE
FREAKY FREYBUG

Re-thunk and illustrated by Franky A. Brown

A long time ago in ~~a galaxy~~ FREAKY *far, far away . . .*

In the blistering heat of the midday sun,
A crowd gathered in Freaky Square.
A shadow was cast by the moon as it passed
And it fell over everyone there.

They cheered and high-fived at the sky with glee
At the annual eclipse celebration,
But there was something in the dark,
With a deep, dreadful bark,
That looked like this
AWESOME *illustration . . .*

'It's a lion, it's a bear, it's a monster!' they cried,

For this DOG was no poodle or pug.

As it prowled through the streets,

Looking for something to eat,

Someone screamed, 'IT'S THE FREAKY FREYBUG!'

Its fur was as black as the shadow of the moon,

Its eyes were as bright as the sun,

And the thick grey fog that surrounded the dog

Scared the pants off everyone!

MY PANTS!
WHERE HAVE
THEY GONE?!

The moon soon cleared and the sun returned

And thankfully no one was eaten!

But not a year goes by when the shadow in the sky

Doesn't bring back the Freaky dog-demon!

Each year it appears, as the sun goes black,

Each year looking hungrier and thinner,

So find somewhere to hide, stay at home, stay inside,

Or you might become the Freaky Freybug's DINNER!

So Freaky legend has it that the Freaky Freybug is not some kind of weird bug like I first thought, but a

GIANT DOG.

And it can only appear and hunt for food during the blackout of a solar eclipse. Apparently, there used to be LOADS of sightings of this giant dog, but he's not been seen for years now.

Pretty scary stuff, right? Well, Jamelia certainly thought it was, but then Jamelia's scared of EVERYTHING. She even made a list once.

Jamelia Pointer's scary list of scary things

The dark: SCARY.

Clowns: SUPER SCARY.

Creakers: TERRIFYING!

The sound of the Hoover: PETRIFYING!

Freaky Freybug: HORRIFYING!

Despite it appearing on Jamelia's list, everyone else laughed when Miss Tinky read the poem, as though it was all just a load of tish-tosh.

Jamelia shook her head. 'It CAN'T be tish-tosh,' she told us all. 'I KNOW that the Freaky Freybug is real.'

'How?' asked Ronnie.

'*Because the Freaky Freybug* ATE A FRIEND OF MY GREAT-GRANDAD'S COUSIN'S UNCLE *during the total eclipse of eighteen ninety-two!*' Jamelia shrieked.

TOTAL TISH-TOSH, RIGHT?

Everyone agreed, and so we forgot about the scary giant dog that could potentially slink out of the shadows to eat us during the eclipse, and spent the rest of the class learning about how eclipses work. Here's a little diagram to show you.

I guess this is easy for us to know now with super-awesome telescopes and satellites to help figure it out, but back in ancient times, before there were computers or cars, when our parents were young, it must have been proper scary stuff. Imagine just walking along when suddenly the whole sky turns black and the sun goes out like a light! No wonder people got spooked by stories about giant dogs that lurk in the shadows!

Anyway, Jamelia spent the whole lesson on edge, looking over her shoulder in case a giant black hound crept up on her. Ronnie barked like a dog, which made Jamelia fall off her chair with fright. Most of the kids in class thought it was super hilarious. I felt pretty bad for her, but I did think she was being a bit silly, believing that old story. I MEAN, GIANT DOGS? AS IF!

Little did we all know that Jamelia would have the last laugh.

When **ECLIPSE DAY** came, there was such a buzz around the school. Everyone had been making these special viewing boxes so we could watch the eclipse without damaging our eyeballs.

Mum wouldn't help me with mine. I asked her to, obviously.

'No one ever did my homework for me, Franky. I used my own initiative,' she told me as she dished out spaghetti and meatballs for dinner.

EASY FOR HER TO SAY. SHE'S AN INVENTOR!

I'm just a kid who doesn't listen properly, so mine ended up looking like this . . .

But it passed Miss Tinky's safety test, so I was allowed to use it. (And I forgave Mum pretty quickly because of the spaghetti and meatballs, YUM.)

School finished early and the whole school marched along the bank of the glistening green water of Lake Freaky, all the way to the old town square, to watch the eclipse. The school band (McFREAKY) were even playing, which made the whole thing feel like a great BIG FESTIVAL!

Ronnie figured out a way of making a little extra money to spend in the tuck shop.

ECLIPSE FEST T-SHIRTS!

I wish I'd thought of it first, plus those T-shirts were super cool and selling out fast. I asked Mum if I could get one, which was a **BIG MISTAKE** because she shut down Ronnie's whole business and made him give all the money back.

The good news was that Mum confiscated the leftover stock so I've got a whole box of Eclipse Fest T-shirts now. I'm going to keep them in the box and sell them in forty years when they're vintage, like Dad's band T-shirts that look (and smell) about a thousand years old!

All of a sudden, everyone started this big countdown and had their eclipse-viewing devices at the ready.

TEN . . .

NINE . . .

EIGHT . . .

SEVEN . . .

SIX . . .

FIVE . . .

FOUR . . .

THREE . . .

TWO . . .

It felt like New Year's Eve, except when we reached **ONE** there wasn't any cheering and kissing . . . just silence, as everyone watched the black moon start blocking out the sun.

It was super awesome seeing the moon make the middle of the day look like the middle of the night. The whole town watched as the shadow fell over us like a blanket of darkness, and I couldn't help but notice that this shadow had a slight hint of green to it.

IT WAS IN THIS GREEN, SHADOWY SILENCE THAT I FIRST HEARD THE GROWL.

My friends and I all looked at each other. I could tell that they'd heard the same thing.

But it wasn't Ronnie Nutbog's bum that had growled. It was something **FAR WORSE.**

FAR LOUDER.

FAR FREAKIER.

Then a thick fog came from nowhere, covering the whole square. Except it was thicker than normal fog . . . more like **SMOKE!**

Then we **SMELLED** it. The unmistakable whiff of dog's breath. IT WAS HOT AND CLOSE!

Then we **FELT** it. Thick, matted fur brushed past us all as though we were sheep being circled by a hungry wolf.

Suddenly it appeared before us in a flash of green . . .

Its eyes were as bright as the sun . . .

Then we saw its dark fur against the white fog . . .

Its fur was as black as the shadow of the moon . . .

And we knew there was only one explanation . . .

Jamelia ripped her eclipse box from her eyes and screamed:

IT'S THE FREAKY FREYBUG!!!

Of course, from then on, it was **TOTAL CHAOS!** Everyone ran around screaming in the dark and in the fog, trying not to be eaten by a giant dog! There wasn't a single thing the teachers could do about it. If I hadn't been so scared about being eaten alive, it would have been pretty awesome!

Every so often, I caught glimpses of the beast as people ran for their lives. I saw:

GROWLING AND RUNNING . . .

BARKING AND SHOVING . . .

TAIL-WAGGING AND SCREAMING . . .

WAIT.

Tail-wagging? That didn't seem very scary!

I looked again and saw a sloppy tongue flapping happily around . . .

That wasn't very scary either!

As the fog cleared a little, I finally got a proper look at this enormous creature. It was a dog all right, but it wasn't hunting for humans . . .

IT WAS **CHASING** ITS OWN TAIL!

PAH-HA-HA!

The laugh blurted out of my mouth – I couldn't help it! Dogs are just too funny! (RIP, Billy.)

But the Freybug heard, and its glowing green eyeballs found me.

I thought I was done for! The dog bounded over to me, galloping like a huge horse across the square. It leaped into the air, its mouth wide open, ready to

SWALLOW ME WHOLE!

But it didn't. It landed on top of me, pinning me down with its lion-like paws, and licked my face like an enormous happy puppy! Its tongue was like one of those massive dead fish you see behind the counter in the supermarket, and it smelled like one too!

DISGUSTING!

While I was happy it wasn't eating me alive (obviously!), there was a chance it was going to slobber me to death if I didn't get this heavy mutt off me!

Suddenly I heard someone's footsteps running towards us.

'You leave my friend alone, you big terrifying dog of my nightmares!' screamed Jamelia, and with that she picked up a huge stick that was lying on the grass.

The Freybug stared at the stick with hungry green eyes. No dog can resist a stick – even a crazy giant dog. IT'S A LAW OF NATURE!

'Franky, get out of there!' Jamelia screamed as the enormous creature crept towards her tempting stick. I rolled out from under its dinner-plate-sized paws just as it launched itself towards Jamelia, and she threw the stick as hard and as far as she could into the thick fog.

I scrambled to my feet, wiping my slobbery face with my sleeves. 'Jamelia, you just saved me from the Freybug! You totally faced your fear!' I said – and I've never seen someone look more proud of themselves.

'Well, I wasn't going to let it eat you!' she said, smiling.

I was about to tell her that actually it had just been licking me and that I thought it was a friendly dog, when we heard a voice calling. We turned, and a strange-looking old man came running out of the fog towards us. He had a long, straggly grey beard, and I thought he looked a bit like a wizard.

HAVE YOU SEEN A GIANT DOG WITH YELLOW EYES AND BLACK FUR?

The old man shook his head, scratched his grey beard and said, 'Oh dear, I'm in trouble now. The sun will be coming out again any minute and we have to be moving on!'

'Hang on! Are you the dog's owner?' I spluttered.

The man chuckled. 'Did that look like a dog with an *owner* to you? No, I'm more of a . . . companion, shall we say.'

'It won't eat anyone, will it?' Jamelia asked, and the man burst out laughing again.

'No, that silly old thing is a firetarian,' he said.

'A *fire*-what?' I replied.

'A FIRETARIAN! It only eats the burning embers of a dying fire. Where do you think all this smoke came from?' he explained, gesturing around.

'Oh, we thought this was FOG!' I said.

'You mean . . . he's not scary?!' Jamelia asked.

'Of course not! He's a big softie! Now, where did he get to?'

'I threw a stick for him, and he ran off to fetch it,' explained Jamelia, and the man shook his head with concern.

'I'm supposed to keep him on his lead, but the poor old thing only gets to go for walkies once a year, so I like to let him have a little run about,' he said. 'I've got a dog whistle for emergencies, but I must have dropped it in all the chaos. I'll never find it on the ground in the dark!'

That's when it hit me. 'MY PENCIL CASE!' I cried.

The man looked puzzled. 'How's that going to help?'

Jamelia grinned at me. 'Franky's pencil case has a –'

'**WHISTLE!**' I smiled.

I quickly opened up my schoolbag and pulled out my Mum-made pencil case. After a few little fiddles, I FOUND THE <u>EMERGENCY WHISTLE!</u>

Well, I blew the whistle and the Freybug came bounding over, puffing smoky fog from its wet nose. The old man held up his hand (I was becoming more and more convinced that he was a wizard) and the dog stopped. The man reached into his pocket and pulled out a smouldering lump of coal.

'Sit . . . lie down . . . stay . . .' he commanded, and the Freybug obeyed. The man shot me and Jamelia a smile. 'You can stroke him if you like.'

The enormous black hound even rolled over and let Jamelia tickle his tummy.

'Well, he must like you!' the old man said and, as the Freybug stood up again, Jamelia was covered in its thick jet-black fur.

'YUCK!' she laughed, trying to pick it off.

'Oh, I'd keep some of that if I were you. It's good luck to have a ball of Freybug fur. Hard to come by too!' said the wizened old man, and Jamelia stuffed a handful into her pocket.

The old man grabbed hold of the Freybug's black fur and leaped up on to its back – a super-cool move!

'Thank you for all your help! What are your names?' he asked.

'I'm Franky Brown and this is Jamelia Pointer,' I said.

'Jamelia Pointer, eh? Well, what do you know? I was friends with your great-grandad's cousin's uncle. Haven't seen him since eighteen ninety-two when I decided to run away and explore the secrets of the eclipse with this giant fleabag,' he said. 'Oh, and cool pencil case, by the way, Franky Brown.'

305

And, with that, he galloped away, following the shadow of the moon.

I suddenly noticed Jamelia looking a little sad.

'What's up?' I asked.

'Nothing really. It's just that earlier on, when I saved you from being eaten, I thought I was being really brave – but it turns out the Freybug wasn't trying to eat you after all.'

'Yeah, but you didn't know that, and you STILL came to the rescue when everyone else ran away. That's pretty awesome if you ask me,' I said, and Jamelia couldn't help the little smile that flashed across her face.

NOT AGAIN! AND I THOUGHT THOSE POOPS ON OUR STREET WERE BAD!

The shadow of the eclipse soon passed and, when the sun returned, everyone found us standing in the middle of the empty square. Well, it was empty except for the enormous pile of FREYBUG POOP.

Obviously, as soon as we got back to Danger Gang headquarters afterwards, Jamelia and I told everyone about the Freybug and the old man and how **MY PENCIL CASE** saved the day, and we crowded round the ball of jet-black Freybug fur that Jamelia fished out of her pocket.

'AWESOME!' we all said admiringly.

Only Mollie was a little quiet. When I asked her what was up, she said, 'Does anyone else get the feeling that all these weird things happening in Freaky might mean something?'

'THE GREEN FLASHES . . .' added Charlie.

'JUST LIKE THAT WEIRD STORM . . .' said Suzy.

'And has anyone else seen some weird shadows lurking around . . . without people attached to them?' asked Eric.

 we all said together.

'Well, whatever's going on, I can't imagine we'll have to deal with anything freakier than a giant fire-eating dog that lives in the shadow of an eclipse,' sighed Jamelia, relaxing into the hammock (a new addition to the Danger Gang treehouse!).

Everyone agreed about that and we celebrated the peak of freakiness with a jar of sherbet flying saucers from Charlie's mum's shop.

I hope you enjoyed the eclipse too. Let me know if you saw the Freybug back in Greyville!

FRANKY

PS Still no new shadow sighting, but in bed last night I heard the STRANGEST NOISE ON THE ROOF. Almost like the footsteps of someone sneaking around.

OCTOBER

Dear Dani,

You won't believe what happened in Freaky this month. I mean, it's strange enough here at the best of times, but throw **HALLOWEEN** into the mix and this place is off the scale!

Freaky has an annual **PUMPKIN COMPETITION** to see who can grow the biggest one. Suzy, who lives over the road from me at Number 8, well, her mum and dad grow **MASSIVE** pumpkins and enter every year. They're easily the best in town. The trouble is, they just can't agree on *how* to grow the best and biggest pumpkin!

Mr Prune thinks you need to plant them in a bucket and water them with a watering can.

Mrs Prune thinks they grow bigger if you plant them in the greenhouse and use a spray bottle to water them.

Neither of them will budge on their pumpkin-growing plans. So they now enter the Pumpkin Competition separately. Which means, each year, only **ONE** of them gets to win the trophy.

Suzy said that this year her dad was feeling super confident about his pumpkin. Apparently, he's got something pretty special up his sleeve. The trouble is, Suzy's mum said that **SHE** has something pretty special up **HER** sleeve this year too.

It's Suzy I feel sorry for, because her mum and dad spend more time with their **PRECIOUS PUMPKINS** than they do with their daughter!

TO MAKE THINGS EVEN WORSE,

over the past few weeks, both of them have been so obsessed with watering, pruning, trimming, and whatever else you do with pumpkins to make them grow, that neither Mr nor Mrs Prune remembered Suzy's birthday.

The Pumpkin Competition was held on Halloween Night. I went trick-or-treating first with Dad before meeting the gang at Freaky Square.

EVERYONE HAD AWESOME

HALLOWEEN COSTUMES . . .

EVERYONE EXCEPT ME.

Dad, as usual, forgot that it was **HIS** job to get my Halloween costume ready, so five minutes before we left the house he fashioned *this* costume together with things he found in the kitchen . . .

SPATULA

COUNT SPATULA

RED TEA TOWEL

ANOTHER SPATULA

SPATULA

I know what you're thinking: why do my parents need **THREE** SPATULAS? And I'm afraid I don't have an answer to that.

Needless to say, I removed the costume the first chance I got and found the rest of the Danger Gang near the front of the crowd that had gathered in Freaky Square.

'Nice costumes!' I said as Mollie made her entire head disappear, terrifying a group of Year Three kids.

Jamelia had come as the **FREAKY FREYBUG**, complete with glowing green eyes (swimming goggles with glow-in-the-dark paint).

Katy showed up as the **MERMAID** from Freaky Falls in a wiry green wig and home-made tail.

Eric had a **CARDBOARD SHARK** head so no one would notice the difference if it rained and he turned into an actual shark.

Charlie came covered in rubbish and said he was a **CREAKER**.

And everyone thought Ronnie's **FRANKENSTEIN** mask was **SUPER REALISTIC** until they realized he wasn't actually wearing a mask . . .

OK, that's probably a bit mean. Frankenstein's monster is <u>**WAY BETTER LOOKING**</u> than Ronnie Nutbog!

'Where's Suzy?' I asked, realizing she was the only one of our Danger Gang missing. But no one had seen her.

When it was time for the pumpkin unveiling, three very important-looking officials came out and introduced themselves as the judging panel. Piers Snoregan off the telly was there, reporting with his film crew, so I'm one step closer to being RICH AND FAMOUS.

I slipped away from the gang to look for Suzy, and found her hiding round the back of the stage.

'Hey, they're about to start the judging,' I said.

'Great!' she said with a sigh, and then took a HUGE bite out of a HUGE slice of pumpkin pie.

'What's up?' I asked.

'I'm just bored of watching Mum and Dad try to outdo each other with stupid, orange . . . *delicious* pumpkins,' she said, taking another gulp of stupid, orange, delicious pumpkin pie. 'Want some?' she asked.

I shook my head. 'No thanks, I'm stuffed. Mum bought a box of twelve doughnuts for trick-or-treaters and I accidentally ate seven when she wasn't looking. But I guess one of your parents is about to win the big trophy. That's pretty cool, right?'

'Yeah, that's awesome **FOR <u>ONE</u> OF THEM**, but that means the other one's going to lose,' she said.

'Oh yeah, that sucks,' I realized, as Suzy gobbled another mouthful of pumpkin pie. 'I'd slow down if I were you or you'll turn into a pumpkin!' I joked as she scoffed the pie.

'Well, at least Mum and Dad might notice me then!' She laughed and finished off the gooey orange slice of pie before we both headed back to watch the unveiling.

There were seven entries in total, including Miss Tinky and the man who sells me nutter-crunches from his ice-cream van, but it was clear to everyone that only two people stood a chance of winning.

First up was Suzy's mum's pumpkin. It was so big it had to be carried out on a **FORKLIFT TRUCK!**

The Freaky crowd burst into applause. All the judges were scribbling notes on their clipboards, nodding their heads, and Mrs Prune was beaming. Piers Snoregan announced, 'In my opinion, this **HAS** to be the winning pumpkin, because this has to be the biggest pumpkin **IN THE WORLD**. In fact, unless anyone can prove that pumpkins grow on other planets, this also has to be the **BIGGEST PUMPKIN IN THE UNIVERSE!**'

But, as usual, his opinion turned out to be utter rubbish. The ground started to rumble and searchlights suddenly lit up the dusky sky, and found something enormous, something round, something orange, flying through the air, being hoisted in by a giant crane over the rooftops and trees!

Suzy sighed. 'Here comes my dad's pumpkin!'

AND WE ALL LOOKED UP IN <u>AMAZEMENT</u>.

319

FREAKY WENT NUTS!

Everyone threw their trick-or-treat bags into the air in celebration as the second gigantic pumpkin was lowered into place next to Mrs Prune's entry. Mr Prune was looking very smug, and avoiding his wife's glare.

Piers Snoregan ran over to get an exclusive interview with the Prunes.

'Mr Prune, how on earth did you manage to grow a pumpkin THIS big? What's your secret?' Piers asked.

'Well, I planted it a little earlier than usual this year, back in March, on the night of that big storm . . .' Mr Prune answered.

'And what about you, Mrs Prune?' demanded Piers.

'So did I!' she replied.

THE MOMENT I HEARD THAT, MY HEART STOPPED.

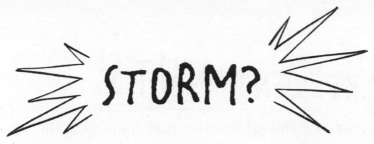

STORM?

If that storm had anything to do with these pumpkins, then we were in for something **FREAKY**.

'Well, I think, for the first year ever, we have a tie!' said Piers Snoregan, looking at the two equally enormous pumpkins. 'You are joint winners and can share the Freaky Pumpkin Competition trophy!'

'Hold on just a tick!' screeched Mrs Prune. 'My pumpkin is clearly the biggest.'

'Don't be daft,' Mr Prune added. 'Your silly little pumpkin is nowhere near as big as mine!'

Then Mrs Prune reached into her gardening utility belt and unclipped a bottle of spray, which I could see was full up with a murky green liquid labelled **RAINWATER!**

'What's that?' Mr Prune asked.

'This is water I collected from the storm on the night MY pumpkin was planted,' said Mrs Prune.

'And what are you going to do with that?' Mr Prune asked, sounding a little nervous.

'I don't think mine has finished growing yet!' Mrs Prune screeched, and with that she went to spray her pumpkin with the freaky storm water.

'Oh no you don't – that's cheating!' cried Mr Prune, and he lunged for the bottle. He tugged it this way, and his wife pulled it that way.

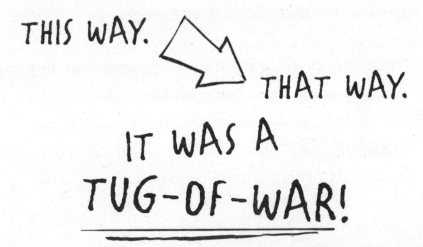

THIS WAY. THAT WAY. IT WAS A TUG-OF-WAR!

'I can't watch this!' Suzy said miserably, and she took a large bite from another piece of pumpkin pie.

At that very moment, the spray bottle full of freaky storm water couldn't take being pulled any longer.

It snapped open and pinged out of Suzy's mum and dad's hands. It flew through the air, soaking poor Suzy with the murky water inside.

Suzy gasped as water dripped from her hair and clothes. I could tell this was the final straw.

'That's enough!' she screamed. 'I've had it with you two and this STUPID COMPETITION!'

As Suzy shouted, I couldn't help but notice the green sparks, like tiny bolts of lightning, that zapped round her body. I whispered to myself, '*It's Danger Time!*'

— AND I WAS RIGHT!

'You spend so much time watching your silly little pumpkins grow that you didn't even notice that I grew . . . a whole year!' Suzy went on.

'Oh, Suzypie, your birthday!' Mrs Prune gasped.

'You forgot her birthday?' asked Mr Prune, looking at his wife in horror.

'*You* did too, Dad!' bellowed Suzy.

'Did I?' he said.

But, while Suzy's mum and dad had failed to remember her growing another year older, I had definitely not failed to notice that she seemed to be growing now – right before our very eyes.

YES, YOU READ THAT CORRECTLY.

SUZY.

WAS.

GROWING!

'Suzy, you're . . . getting bigger!' Ronnie shouted.

'And your skin is turning orange!' added Katy.

And it was! Suzy wasn't just plumping up like someone was inflating her with a bike pump. She was actually turning orange!

BIGGER AND **BIGGER.**
ROUNDER AND **ROUNDER!**

Until she was as big as her mum and dad's prize-winning pumpkins, and the same colour too!

'My Suzypie!' Mr Prune cried. 'You're a . . . you're a . . .'

'A PUMPKIN!' her mum screamed at Suzy's round orange face poking out of the top of an even rounder, more orange body!

The whole town started screaming and running for their lives.

'PUMPKIN MONSTER!' they cried.

'KILLER SUPER SQUASH!' they yelled.

Suzy, the now-giant pumpkin, lifted up one of her ginormous pumpkin feet and took a stomping pumpkin step forward.

The ground shook. It was like watching one of those old films where Godzilla fights those awesome giant monsters in the middle of the city. If Godzilla had to fight Pumpkin Suzy, I'm not sure who would win!

'Suzypie, we can fix you!' Mr Prune cried.

'Yes, your dad is brilliant at making pumpkins small!' Mrs Prune said.

'Oi!'

'Well, you are!' she replied.

'STOP ARGUING ABOUT PUMPKINS!'

Suzy bellowed, and with that she lifted up her heavy orange foot and brought it crashing down on top of her mum's prize-worthy pumpkin.

The pumpkin was PULVERIZED and chunks of orange flesh splattered over the watching, chaotic crowd.

'Pah-ha-ha!' Mr Prune cackled at the sight. 'Looks like the trophy is all mine this year!'

But giant Pumpkin Suzy had different plans. She lifted up her other round orange foot and smashed her dad's pumpkin to bits!

Now I'm not sure exactly how what happened next happened, but the moment those pumpkins were smashed open it was almost as if a spell had been broken. Just like when a hypnotist snaps his fingers and wakes someone up who's been prancing around like a chicken a moment before, Mr and Mrs Prune instantly changed.

'Oh, my Suzypie!' said Mrs Prune.

'My little . . . I mean, **BIG** girl!' sobbed Mr Prune.

They both wrapped their arms round their little, big pumpkin-girl's legs and cried, and cried, and cried. And, as their teardrops trickled down their cheeks and on to the orange flesh of their pumpkin-girl, some sort of magic transformation began. Instead of watering a plant to make it grow, their tears were making Suzy shrink.

DOWN, **DOWN**, **DOWN** she went, getting smaller and smaller, and less and less orange, until Suzy was SUZY again.

'Our Suzypie!' Mr and Mrs Prune cheered.

Suzy was back, but now we had another problem. A **BIGGER** PROBLEM! Everyone in Freaky had just seen giant Pumpkin Suzy stomping around town like a monster from one of those old B-movies!

There was **NO WAY** we were going to be able to keep this a secret within the Danger Gang. And not only that – Piers Snoregan and his TV crew were there. This was going to go viral!

'She's done for!' Charlie whispered as the Danger Gang reconvened.

'She'll be taken away for all sorts of scientific testing, for sure!' said Mollie.

'Or locked up for being a danger to society!' added Ronnie.

As Piers Snoregan and the crew rushed over to her, we all thought this might be the last we'd ever see of our friend Suzy Prune. But Piers suddenly burst into hysterical laughter, clapping and cheering wildly.

'YOUNG LADY, THAT WAS THE BEST HALLOWEEN COSTUME I HAVE EVER SEEN!'

he roared. 'I don't know how on earth you made it, but what a treat it was. Or was it a TRICK? Pa-ha-ha!'

The stunned crowd, who had been screaming in terror moments before, suddenly erupted into applause.

I looked around at the Danger Gang, and we all joined in cheering!

'WHOOPEE! WHAT A COSTUME!' we cried.

'LOOKED FAKE TO ME,' Ronnie heckled.

'YEAH, YOU COULD SEE THE ZIP!' Eric laughed.

'DIDN'T BELIEVE IT FOR A SECOND,' Katy yelled.

'I think everyone here can safely say that you, Suzy Prune, were the biggest "pumpkin" any of us has ever seen!' Piers Snoregan chuckled as he pinned the First Place rosette on her jumper. 'And there's no way a Halloween costume like that was made without the help of Mum and Dad, so I suppose the JOINT winners of this year's Freaky Pumpkin Prize are

MR AND MRS PRUNE!'

I felt the Danger Gang breathe a sigh of relief and we said nothing else about it until we were safely within the wooden walls of my treehouse later that evening.

So that was my Freaky Halloween, but to be honest I expected nothing less!

HAPPY TRICK-OR-TREATING!

FRANKY

PS PHOTOGRAPHIC EVIDENCE!

Take a look at the picture of Mr and Mrs Prune with their winning entry – Suzy! Notice anything unusual? Count the people, then count the shadows . . . SOMEONE ELSE WAS THERE!

DANI!

I'M IN <u>TROUBLE!</u>

Something ~~REALLY~~ ~~MEGA~~ ~~SUPER~~
FREAKISHLY FREAKY has happened and I don't think
I'm going to make it! This is my final letter, my last
goodbye and there's something you need to know.
There's no easy way to say this, but I . . .

I LOVE YOU, DANI!

I knew you were the one for me since the day we first
met and I caught you eating your bogey at the back of
the classroom. IT WAS LOVE AT FIRST BITE!

Don't try to save me and, whatever you do, don't come
to Freaky – it's too dangerous here. Maybe even for the
Danger Gang.

<u>FRANKY</u> — over and out.

Dear Dani,

HOW FUNNY WAS MY LAST LETTER?

PAH-HA-HA.

You know I wasn't being serious, right? I'm such a joker these days.

♡ ♡

What am I like! I was all '*I love you . . .*' and stuff.

TOTALLY
NOT TRUE.

I mean, you're cool and everything, and still my best friend, but have I been 'in love' with you since the second we met?

OF COURSE NOT!

Remembered every detail of your smile?

AS IF!

Do I know the specific shape of the eight tiny moles on your face (that you hate, but I think are ~~awesome~~ nice)?

I didn't even know you had eight moles!

We're just mates, all right?

Anyway, according to your last letter, which I've just read, you have a BOYFRIEND now. That's *soooo* great. I'm **REALLY HAPPY** for you. Have you held his hand yet?

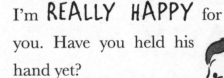

GROSS!

Not that I care or anything. I just want to know because WE'RE FRIENDS!

My last letter was mostly jokes about me loving you, but something FREAKISHLY FREAKY actually did happen and I wasn't sure if I was going to make it. I'd better tell you what happened.

I was in class, about to write the date on the top of my page, when, through the classroom window, I saw a van pulling up in the school car park. It looked like an ordinary van, but something about the logo on the side felt really familiar.

Then I remembered that name: SHADOW TECH. It was the science company my mum used to work for before they fired her!

I thought it was weird that they were in the car park of my new school, and then I saw a man get out and open the back of the van. From the classroom, I couldn't get a good look at his face. It was half in shadow, and he was wearing **REALLY** dark sunglasses that covered up his features.

IN NOVEMBER!

SUSPICIOUS, RIGHT?

If there was ever a guy who was up to no good, IT WAS THIS ONE.

He looked just like Dr Vendetta. Seriously, my heart stopped when I saw him! I was all like, **NO WAY!** and then my brain was like, *Chill out, Franky. Dr Vendetta isn't real!* and I was like, *Oh yeah! Thanks!* But this guy was so OBVIOUSLY a baddie that I quickly drew this sketch of him in case I needed it for evidence later.

JET-BLACK HAIR, →
SLICKED BACK

— SUNGLASSES TO HIDE HIS
FACE (THE BEST DISGUISE!)

EARPIECE TO
COMMUNICATE WITH
OTHER BADDIES . . .

REALLY SMART SUIT

FINGERLESS GLOVES . . .
ALL BAD GUYS
WEAR THOSE!

SEE WHAT I MEAN! He was one hundred per cent a bad guy – I could just tell. But what was he doing in Freaky?

Suddenly my mind started to piece things together, like it was doing a puzzle:

MUM GETS FIRED FROM TECH COMPANY.

MUM MOVES AWAY FROM TECH COMPANY.

MUM GETS NEW JOB AT SCHOOL
IN NEW TOWN.

TECH COMPANY SHOWS UP AT NEW SCHOOL
IN NEW TOWN . . .

Which can only mean one thing: **SHADOW TECH** must be looking for Mum!

Then I remembered those weird shadows I'd been seeing all year, and the feeling that I was being watched. What if Shadow Tech have been spying on me?

WELL, NOT ON ME, BUT ON MUM
AND HER INVENTIONS!

Now I'm no expert, but if I was a tech company I wouldn't be bothered about the KID-SHUTTER-UPPER or the HUSBAND-O-SHHHH. I *would*, however, be extremely interested in a device that could control the weather.

A DEVICE LIKE THE ONE THAT WAS SITTING IN OUR GARAGE!

What if – and you'll have to go with me on this, Dani – what if Shadow Tech was actually not a very nice company? Mum did say that some of the people were 'trouble' and 'not to be trusted'. In fact, what if they were EVIL? And what if this EVIL company realized they could use Mum's weather-zapping invention to take control of the planet's weather systems?

THINK ABOUT IT! If Shadow Tech could control the weather, they could probably use the WEATHER RAY's weather-zapping technology for their own evil ends! Now I don't know exactly what evil ends Shadow Tech have yet, but, if this guy in the car park who looked JUST like Dr Vendetta was anything to go by, it's probably

TAKING OVER THE WORLD

OR

BLOWING UP THE MOON

OR

DESTROYING ALL THE DOUGHNUT BAKERIES!

Yeah, that would probably be the worst one: ridding the world of doughnuts!

While I was doodling that awesome picture, I kept one eye on the Shadow-Tech guy and saw him walk round the other side of his van. BUT, when he appeared at the back, he had changed.

And I'm not talking about his clothes. I mean, he had TRANSFORMED.

And I'm not talking about into a werewolf or anything. This is *real life*, Dani!

The *Shadow-Tech* baddie had become a SHADOW!

At first, I thought he was waiting on the other side of the van, but then I saw it. The clear dark shadow of him. With NO PERSON ATTACHED TO IT.

I had just seen proof that those shadows I'd been seeing all year were real. They were this guy!

I TOLD YOU!

Don't ask me how he transformed into a shadow in the first place. I don't have the foggiest idea, but Mum used to say that all sorts of weird technology was invented at Shadow Tech . . . and, since *shadow* is in their name, I guess they've got some super-awesome baddie gadget that can transform them at the swish of a wand. No, wait, that's wizards . . . a flick of a switch. Yeah, that's more like it. A SHADOW-MAKER 3000 (that's what I'd call it). WISH I HAD ONE OF THOSE!

But why was this shadow now dashing through the school car park? I watched it scurry round the cars, zip across the empty spaces and head straight towards the main entrance. I had to rub my eyes to check I wasn't imagining things, because it was super weird seeing someone's shadow when the *someone* wasn't there.

If Shadow Tech was after one of my mum's inventions and one of them was here in Freaky, at my SCHOOL, then they must know that Mum works here.

I HAD TO WARN HER!

I put my hand up and asked to go to the loo, but Miss Tinky said what she always says. 'You should have gone before my class started, Franky Brown. Hold it in.'

SOOOOO ANNOYING!

THAT SHADOW WAS GETTING AWAY!

'Please, Miss Tinky!' I begged.

'No.'

'But I'll wet myself!'

'If you must.'

My friends were staring at me by now. They must have been wondering what I was up to, but there just wasn't time to explain. I'm ashamed to admit it, but I genuinely tried to pee my pants . . . just a little bit, enough so that she'd send me to lost property to get some new trousers.

But I couldn't do it! I didn't need to pee! When you've gotta go, you've gotta go . . .

AND WHEN YOU DON'T, YOU JUST DON'T!

I needed another way to get out of class, and FAST –
so I did something dangerous, *seriously* dangerous.

Sticking out of Ronnie's jacket pocket was a can of
Apple Fizzplosion, his very favourite fizzy drink. Those
things were LOADED with sugar and there's no way
anyone's parents would let kids drink them, including
Ronnie's, which is why he always had one secretly
stashed away in his jacket pocket so he could take little
sips when Miss Tinky wasn't looking.

I could see that he hadn't opened it yet, but I knew
it wouldn't be long before he did, so I 'accidentally'
dropped my pencil on the floor, and gave it a little nudge
towards Ronnie's desk with my foot.

I quietly walked over to get it, and as I crouched down
to pick it up I whispered, 'It's Danger Time.' Then I
secretly slipped the Apple Fizzplosion out of Ronnie's
pocket and

SHOOK IT!

It wasn't just any old shake. I really went for it, Dani, and when I was done I managed to slip it back into his jacket pocket without Ronnie noticing a thing.

I SAT BACK AT MY SEAT AND WAITED.

AND WAITED.

AND GOT BORED OF WAITING.

So I used my special mind powers and planted an idea in Ronnie's head. I leaned back casually in my seat and said to my gang, 'Hmmm, I'm thirsty. Is anyone else thirsty?'

'Quiet, please, Franky Brown!' called Miss Tinky.

OK, it wasn't quite Jedi-mind-trick-worthy, but it worked! A few moments later, Ronnie checked Miss Tinky wasn't looking and reached for the can in his pocket.

'Pssst! You might want to hide under your desk for a second,' I whispered to Eric.

'Why?' he replied.

'Just trust me,' I said, putting my hand on my head like a shark fin.

'Oh!' He nodded and slid under his desk just as Ronnie slipped the can out of his pocket, placed his fingernail under the ring and . . .

Let's just say that Apple Fizzplosion lived up to its name.

THE EXPLOSION WAS
COLOSSAL!

I mean, I've never seen anything like it. It was on the ceiling and everything! Most importantly though, we were all soaked (apart from Eric, thanks to my warning). Me, Mollie, Charlie, Jamelia, Suzy, Katy and, of course, Ronnie!

IT WORKED!

'Go and get dried off, all of you, and then I will need an explanation,' Miss Tinky told us crossly, and we marched out of the classroom, along with a totally dry Eric, who was pretending to wring out his shirt.

The second we were in the corridor, Charlie said, 'What was **THAT** all about?!'

'It was my fault!' I explained. 'I shook up the can of Apple Fizzplosion. I'm really sorry, but **I HAD TO DO IT**. Something's happening and I think my mum might be in danger! Remember those weird shadows we've all been seeing?'

Quickly, I explained what I had spotted out of the classroom window. Luckily, the idea of being on a top-secret mission to warn my mum that a mysterious evil shadow-agent was in the school to try and steal one of her inventions stopped Ronnie from boshing me on the nose. (Although I do have to buy him a new can of Apple Fizzplosion.)

We ran through the corridors and got to the science lab just in time to spot a dark shadow entering the classroom and the door closing behind it.

I don't know if my friends had completely believed me up until they saw the shadow for themselves, because suddenly they *weren't* so keen on being involved in my top-secret mission to intercept an evil shadow-agent. I could see that they were all nervous. Katy was biting her lip, Ronnie had gone very pale, and Mollie was twitching her nose like a frightened rabbit.

Suddenly I realized what Mollie was doing.

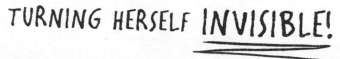

TURNING HERSELF INVISIBLE!

'Great idea, Mollie!' I whispered. 'Once you're invisible, you can sneak into my mum's class and see if you can find that Shadow-Tech *shadow*!'

Everyone else agreed, although I think it was mainly because if Mollie did it then they wouldn't have to!

'What are you lot going to do?' she asked.

'We'll watch through the window,' I replied.

So we did, and I'll admit that watching an invisible girl spy on a shadow isn't the most exciting thing I've ever seen . . .

But, just when I was starting to doubt whether or not I had really seen an evil shadow-agent, the bell rang for lunchbreak and all the kids rushed out of Mum's classroom. Mollie reappeared in the crowd heading to the cafeteria.

'I saw the shadow STEAL something from your mum's desk,' she whispered.

'What was it?' I asked, but before Mollie could answer Mum was standing next to us!

'What are you doing here? Is everything OK?' she asked.

I was about to tell her the truth. I really was.

But instead I said, 'Yep. Everything's fine.'

Because, right at that moment, over Mum's shoulder, Eric was pointing at something! It was the shadow slinking away, and I instantly realized what he'd STOLEN FROM HER DESK!

MUM'S HOUSE KEYS!

It was **SO** freaky, because Mum's house keys weren't floating in the air. He wasn't invisible, like Mollie. The actual shadow was HOLDING the keys!

IT WAS LIKE THE SHADOW WAS ALIVE!

I quickly waved goodbye to Mum and sprinted through the hallways, chasing after the shadow with the footsteps of my friends close behind me. He must have known we were after him, because his shadow started to run.

And, as he ran, the keys
SLID ACROSS THE FLOOR,

THEN UP THE WALL,

sometimes even **ON THE CEILING**
– depending on where the shadow went!

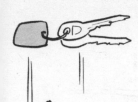

Then we got lucky. As the shadow shot round a corner, Mum's keys caught on a coat hook.

'I'VE GOT 'EM!' Ronnie yelled as he grabbed the dangling keys – then, all of a sudden, the hallway grew VERY DARK. It was like the shadow was expanding, growing, covering everything.

RUN!!

We ran as fast as we could, throwing the keys to each other whenever we felt shadowy hands reaching for us!

Just as I sensed the shadowy hands getting close to me, I threw the keys across the hallway, but Suzy missed them and they slid under the door to – the GIRLS' TOILETS.

Katy, Suzy, Mollie and Jamelia burst in and the shadow followed!

I didn't know what to do. I mean, this was THE GIRLS' TOILETS. I looked at Ronnie. He looked at Eric. Eric looked at Charlie, and then us boys looked at the floor. We didn't want to go in *there*! Who knows what happens in that place? There are more unanswered questions about THE GIRLS' TOILETS than there are about the depths of a

But then I thought about the girls, our friends, and the shadow, and the Apple Fizzplosion that I'd soaked them with. They were only here because of me – I couldn't leave them to handle this alone! So I had to do the scariest thing I've done so far in Freaky and go into THE GIRLS' TOILETS!

I knew I might never come back out again, so I quickly scribbled you that letter and popped it in the school postbox (you know, the letter where I was totally joking about being in love with you? Hahaha, so funny! Lol!) AND STEPPED INTO THE UNKNOWN.

The first thing I noticed was that it didn't smell ANYTHING like the boys' toilets. The girls' loos smell like a florist's!

The second thing I noticed was Suzy, crouching under the sink. Then Katy, who was using her gymnastics skill to hide herself up on the pipes in the ceiling. Jamelia had obviously jumped through the window that was partly open (her purple hair bobble was just visible outside) . . . which left Mollie, who I guessed was in the furthest cubicle, judging by the two feet I spotted trembling beneath the door.

The shadow instantly made its way towards the cubicles and started flinging the doors open, one by one!

I thought Mollie was done for! But, when the shadow got to her door and pushed it open,

MOLLIE WAS GONE.

She'd managed to **TURN INVISIBLE**, just in time! Unfortunately, Mum's keys weren't invisible and were sitting on the toilet seat.

So the shadow-baddie snatched them up and shot straight past us, back into the corridor! We chased him, but soon lost him in the crowd of kids coming out for their lunchbreak.

'I need to get home,' I said. 'Tell Miss Tinky I wasn't feeling well or something.'

'No way. I'm coming with you!' said Eric.

'So am I!' Mollie nodded.

'Me too,' agreed Katy.

'Me three!' laughed Suzy.

'Wouldn't miss it!' Charlie grinned.

'Count me in!' Jamelia said.

'I guess it's better than school . . .' Ronnie sighed.

'Are you sure? I mean, it could be dangerous!' I warned them.

'Danger? Then we're definitely coming. We're the Danger Gang, aren't we?' said Suzy.

'**EXACTLY!**' cheered Charlie.

We hopped on our bikes and left lunchtime at school behind, which was

SOOOOOO BAD
BUT SOOOOOO MUCH FUN.

The November sky was already starting to darken at the edges like a photo with some seriously moody filter on it. Our handlebars were as cold as nutter-crunch and the wind whistled like ghosts in the trees as we pedalled through our secret short cut back to Strike Lane. It was like a scene from the kind of movies our parents don't let us watch in case we get any 'funny ideas', but they don't realize that those movies get all their 'funny ideas' from kids like us!

The plan was as follows: go home, stop Shadow Tech from stealing the **WEATHER RAY** and get back to school before lunchbreak was over or we'd all be in *serious* trouble.

The problem was, riding our bikes was so much fun that we sort of forgot about *the plan* and stopped for doughnuts (my totally brilliant idea, of course) . . .

THEN WE WENT TO THE CINEMA . . .

PLAYED AT THE ARCADE . . .

WENT BOWLING...

THEN ICE SKATING...

AND BACK FOR MORE DOUGHNUTS

(my awesome idea again)...

before we realized it was TOTALLY DARK and we'd missed the WHOLE OF AFTERNOON SCHOOL!

By the time we got to my house, the police were there – and my suspicions were proved right. It WAS the **WEATHER RAY** the shadow had been after . . . and it was **GONE**. It was in the hands of Shadow Tech now.

As we crept inside, Mum was giving a statement to a police officer about the break-in and Dad was looking sheepish in the corner. It turns out that Dad was home, looking after Max, when the burglary happened, but didn't hear it **BECAUSE HE WAS ASLEEP**.

When the police officer asked if anything valuable had been taken, and if she had any idea who it could have been, Mum said, 'No, just one of my useless inventions that doesn't even work. I'm quite glad to be rid of it, to be honest. It was starting to smell like old nappies.'

Mum called someone to change the locks, and the gang all headed home. That evening, we ate dinner as if **NOTHING HAD HAPPENED**. As though an **EVIL COMPANY** trying to take over the world (probably), destroy the moon (maybe) and blow up every doughnut bakery (possibly) hadn't just stolen an invention that has the ability to control the weather. I guess Mum and Dad didn't know what we knew about Shadow Tech being in Freaky though. They just thought it had been a random thief.

AS IF!

The Danger Gang all met up in the treehouse later for an official debrief, but the day had been so freaky that we just sat in silence. It was then that my brain started itching a bit, like I'd missed something important and the smart person inside my head was screaming at me, but I wasn't listening. I wasn't sure what it was, but I couldn't help thinking it might have something to do with what Mum had said to the police earlier. Her voice kept echoing in my mind.

'Just one of my useless inventions . . . It was starting to smell like old nappies . . .'

OLD NAPPIES? I had no idea why I kept thinking about that.

What I *did* know was that if Shadow Tech were planning to destroy doughnuts (or take over the world) with Mum's WEATHER RAY, then there was only one group of kids that could stop them . . .

THE DANGER GANG!

So I came up with a new idea.

WE WERE GOING TO TAKE BACK THE WEATHER RAY!

I'm not sure how we're going to do that yet, but whatever we do will be **TOP SECRET**, so don't tell **ANYONE** . . . including your nosy sister and your new 'boyfriend'.

Write back soon if you're not too busy holding hands.

FRANKY

PS I'm really happy for you because you're my best friend and I'm **NOT** in love with you.

DEAR: DANGER DANI
(I'LL EXPLAIN YOUR NEW CODENAME IN A MINUTE)

YOU ARE INVITED TO:
TAKE BACK THE WEATHER RAY

ON: 18 DECEMBER

WHEN: MIDNIGHT

WHERE: THE DANGER GANG WILL ~~RENDEVU~~
~~RONDAYVEW~~ MEET AT SHADOW TECH HQ

FROM: DANGER FRANKY

PS TURN OVER FOR MORE INFO.

Sorry about the LAME party invitation, it was all I could get my hands on. Thanks for replying so fast to my last letter. I know I don't normally write to you twice in a month, but I wanted to sneak this one in before December!

First, I'm SO SORRY to hear that your 'boyfriend' dumped you for Gemma Goldenberg.

I don't know why all the boys back in Greyville like Gemma Goldenberg anyway. I mean, she's not even funny and can't run very fast and I've never seen her climb a tree ONCE!

ANYWAY, ON TO MORE IMPORTANT THINGS . . .

SHADOW TECH!

374

Thank you *soooooo* much for spying on them back in Greyville.

YOU ARE THE BEST!

Good job I did a doodle of the evil baddie guy in my last letter so you knew who to look for. Miss Tinky always tells me off for drawing in class, but I knew it would pay off one day. In your face, Miss Tinky!

Thanks to you, we know that the WEATHER RAY is being kept at Shadow Tech HQ back in Greyville. Therefore we would like to officially invite you to join the

DANGER GANG!

I've checked with the others and told them that you're really cool, so as long as you help us get the WEATHER RAY back . . .

YOU'RE IN.

WELCOME TO THE GANG!

You can cut out this membership card and must keep it on you at all times.

So, as you might have guessed, the Danger Gang is making a secret trip to Greyville to get Mum's invention back before Shadow Tech do something **REALLY** bad with it.

This is going to be the **BIGGEST** top-secret mission of our lives and I have a plan:

THE PLAN!

STEP 1. Fake a sleepover

STEP 2. Escape from Freaky on bikes

STEP 3. Meet you at Shadow-Tech HQ

STEP 4. ~~Steal~~ Take back Mum's **WEATHER RAY**

STEP 5. ~~Kiss you~~ Say goodbye and
return to Freaky as **HEROES**

STEP 6. NEVER TELL ANYONE
ABOUT STEPS 1-5

As you can see, I've thought this all through, and nothing **AT ALL** can possibly go wrong. So, until Friday night, keep your head low and your eyes open. Ooh and I almost forgot – we're all using our super-awesome Danger Gang codenames now. It's basically your name but with the word *Danger* in front of it.

SEE YOU SOON, DANGER DANI!

(Sounds cool, doesn't it? It was my idea!)

FRANKY AKA DANGER FRANKY!

 **DECEMBER**

Dear Danger Dani,

MERRY CHRISTMAS!

Well, I'm not sure where to begin with this letter, except to say

THAT WAS THE
FREAKIEST NIGHT
OF MY LIFE!

There were lasers and guard dogs, helicopters, REAL secret agents and **YOU**. And, of course, that big, super, **MEGA-ENORMOUS TWIST** that none of us saw coming!!!

OK, before I carry on, I guess I should fill you in on all the stuff that happened **BEFORE** we met you at Shadow-Tech HQ!

STEP 1: THE FAKE SLEEPOVER

It was the night of the school Christmas concert and we'd arranged a 'sleepover' at Charlie's house. We chose *his* house because we already knew from his birthday party that his parents can sleep through ANYTHING! I mean, if they could catch some Zs while a giant hamster nearly ate their child, then I had no doubt we'd be able to sneak out of the house unnoticed.

We all pretended to be really sleepy so Mr and Mrs Campbell would send us to bed early. This meant we had to use our best ACTING skills.

OH, IS THAT THE TIME ALREADY?

THINK I'LL BE TURNING IN SOON . . .

BEST BE CATCHING MY FORTY WINKS.

They **TOTALLY** fell for it and let us go to bed at 8 p.m. **AND** because we were camping in the living room again it meant they had to go to bed too and within ten minutes we could hear Mr Campbell snoring!

SO WE SNEAKED OUT AND

STEP 1

OF THE PLAN WAS **COMPLETE!**

STEP 2:
ESCAPE FROM FREAKY ON BIKES

We picked up our bikes, which we'd stashed in the massive town Christmas tree in Freaky Square.

I had pre-packed a backpack full of
ESSENTIAL SUPPLIES.

MINCE PIES

TRIPLE-FUDGE DOUGHNUTS

CHOCOLATE COINS

A SLICE OF LAST NIGHT'S FREAKY PIZZA
(EXTRA CHEESE)

A FLASK OF HOT CHOCOLATE

SPARE SOCKS

A SPORK

A SANTA HAT

A TORCH

ZACK DANGER'S SUPER-SPY'S GUIDE TO SECRET MISSIONS
(THE BEST BOOK EVER!)

AND A TOILET ROLL
(JUST IN CASE)

My backpack was much heavier than I remembered when I lifted it from the tree. I guessed it was because Dad had splashed out on double-quilted loo roll (even though it feels exactly the same on your bum). I threw it on my back anyway and we pedalled like we've never pedalled before!

After what felt like hours of hardcore pedalling through the crunchy, snow-covered streets under the yellowy glow of street lamps, we decided to stop for a snack. Everyone gathered round my backpack as I unzipped it –

AND NEARLY HAD A <u>HEART ATTACK!</u>

I had **NO IDEA** how or when that little chocolate thief Max got in there, but it was too late to take him back home now or we'd fail in our mission. Max wasn't the only backpack stowaway either. I caught Charlie secretly feeding carrot sticks to Mr Fluffles, who was currently in *normal-hamster* form inside his exercise ball.

'What's that rat doing here?' Ronnie barked.

'He's a hamster, not a rat. And I wasn't going to leave him at home. He's my sidekick!' Charlie said, looking lovingly at Mr Fluffles.

As cool as sidekicks are, we now had **TWO** extra living things to worry about on this mission! Our only choice was to make them honorary members of the Danger Gang and push on with slightly fewer snacks, thanks to Max. That sucked – but at least it meant that

STEP 2
WAS COMPLETE!

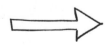

STEP 3:
MEET YOU AT SHADOW-TECH HQ

The ride to Greyville was SO weird. It was like going back in time to my old life. I thought about giving the gang a tour of my former hometown, but just then we heard the town hall clock chime nine, and I knew we had to get to Shadow-Tech HQ as fast as we could – which, thanks to my navigational skills, wasn't that hard to find.

But the moment we got there I knew something was wrong because . . .

YOU WEREN'T THERE!

'Where's Dani?' Ronnie scoffed.

'You said she'd be here!' said Mollie, looking worried.

'I told you she didn't exist! She's just his imaginary girlfriend!' teased Ronnie.

'She's not my girlfriend and she's one hundred per cent real!' I snapped.

'If she *is* real, then she's probably too scared to get involved with top-secret Danger Gang business,' said Ronnie – just as you did that SWEET WHEELIE round the corner.

I wish, wish, wish I had a photo of Ronnie Nutbog's face at that moment.

With you there, **STEP 3** and the Danger Gang were both **COMPLETE** for the first time, and I couldn't help thinking there was suddenly a strange energy in the air around us.

OBVIOUSLY, THAT JUST TURNED OUT TO BE MAX'S NAPPY . . .

Since I didn't know he'd be coming on this mission, I hadn't brought any clean nappies, so we were all just going to have to get used to the new aroma and get on with . . .

STEP 4:
TAKE BACK MUM'S WEATHER RAY

OK, I'LL CONFESS: I had TOTALLY underestimated this step.

There was the drawbridge over the moat filled with deadly piranhas . . .

The first security guard . . .

THE WHOLE CANTEEN FULL OF SECURITY GUARDS . . .

The laser defence system . . .

The cameras . . .

The patrol dogs . . .

IT WAS ALL SUDDENLY LOOKING
IMPOSSIBLE.

'The controls to lower the bridge are on the other side!' you noticed, pointing over the water that was alive with the hungry splashes of the piranhas below.

I totally meant it when I gave the order to

ABORT MISSION!

'There's no way we're getting inside. Let's just go home,' I said sulkily.

'Too late,' said Suzy, staring at the bank of the deadly moat filled with flesh-eating piranhas where a skinny boy was removing his shoes and was about to jump in!

'ERIC, NO!' I cried – but Suzy was right. It *was* too late! Eric dived head first into the black water.

'He's done for!' you screamed, but we all knew he had something up his sleeve.

Suddenly thousands of flesh-eating fish, who would usually look *terrifying*, were leaping out of the water looking TERRIFIED! It was as though they were trying to get away from something.

AND <u>THEY</u> WERE!

Shark-Eric torpedoed across the moat unharmed and shot up the bank on the other side to where the drawbridge controls were. He lowered the large metal bridge and within a minute we'd crossed it.

'That was awesome!' you said, high-fiving Eric.

'Thanks! If you think that's cool, you should see what the others can do,' said Eric (who was now back in human mode!).

As you looked round at the Danger Gang, I could tell we were all thinking the same thing.

'If we all use our freaky abilities . . .' Mollie said,

'And work together . . .' added Suzy,

'Then maybe we could . . .' said Charlie.

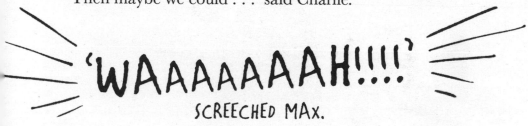

'WAAAAAAAH!!!!'
SCREECHED MAX.

The sound of his cry echoed across the moat and would surely alert someone if we didn't find a way to shut him up!

I tried everything: cooing, singing, biffing myself on the nose, but nothing was working!

'For crying out loud, can you not understand a word he's saying?' snapped Ronnie. 'He wants a snack!'

Charlie quickly reached into his bag, pulled out a carrot stick and handed it to Max, and he stopped crying instantly.

'WAIT! YOU CAN UNDERSTAND HIM?' I GASPED.

Ronnie nodded.

'*You* can understand my baby brother's cry?'

'Yeah! Ever since that freaky thing happened to me in the summer. You know, when you had to change my –'

'We remember!' I said quickly, not wanting to relive it!

'Right. Well, since then, I've been able to understand babies,' Ronnie said, as though this was no big deal!

A few moments later, the Danger Gang was running towards Shadow Tech, ready to face whatever obstacles they put in our way, with my baby brother, silent and smiling, strapped to the back of his new best friend/babysitter . . . RONNIE!

Mollie fooled the first security guard by turning invisible and stealing his keys.

Charlie unscrewed the lid of Mr Fluffles's exercise ball, carefully dropped a few pieces of sweet 'n' salty popcorn inside, screwed the lid back on and rolled the ball into the WHOLE CANTEEN FULL OF SECURITY GUARDS enjoying their coffee break.

We dived for cover outside and heard the shattering of the ball followed by

TERRIFIED SCREAMS

as the security team ran for their lives!

Katy **BACKFLIPPED** through the maze of lasers, squeezing through the tightest of gaps that only someone as tiny as her would have been able to manage, until she was at the other side and disabled them.

I spotted Suzy staring at the security cameras facing us. Then she took a deep breath and HELD IT.

AND HELD IT.

AND HELD IT.

And instead of turning red in the face, like any other kid would, she was turning pumpkin orange! I thought for a second she was going to explode into that huge, round pumpkin like she did on Halloween, but instead her fingers turned as green as a forest and shot out like long, twisting vines, which she used like whips to smash the lenses of the spying cameras.

Jamelia tamed the guard dogs with the Freybug fur that she now kept tied round her wrist as a bracelet, and the fearsome hounds cowered in obedience at the scent of **THE LEGENDARY DOG**.

We were doing it. The plan was actually working. Plus, running through the corridors of Shadow Tech with you was **SO COOL**! I finally had my sidekick back and you're way better than a hamster! It must have been how Batman feels when Robin gets back from holiday.

All we had to do now was find the **WEATHER RAY** and get
out of there. Everything had gone so well that this next
part seemed like it was going to be **EASY-PEASY**!

UNTIL . . .

Katy squeaked and pointed at something moving
up ahead. Something dark and grey on the walls –
A SHADOW!
THEN ANOTHER ONE!
AND ANOTHER . . .

Until there was a whole SQUAD of Shadow-Tech
shadow-guards patrolling the corridor ahead of us and
they all stopped outside
one door.

It looked hopeless. There was no way we were going to get past them. We had already failed against one back at the school and this was a WHOLE SQUAD!

BUT THEN YOU HAD A BRIGHT IDEA.

'What do shadows hate?' you asked.

We all shrugged, and you pulled your torch out of your backpack and flicked it on. 'Light!'

It was an awesome idea, but there was no way one little torch was going to be bright enough to wipe out those shadow-guards. That's when we all whipped out our torches and flicked them on too. I grabbed my trusty pencil-case torch from my rucksack as well and, as I switched it on, I noticed a familiar crackle of green light around it, zapping from the torch's handle and all along my hand . . .

THAT'S WHEN SOMETHING FREAKY HAPPENED IN GREYVILLE!

All the lights in Shadow-Tech HQ dimmed a little, as though the power was being sucked out of them. Then Katy gave another little squeak.

'Franky!' she gasped. 'You're GLOWING!'

I looked down. My hand was pulsing with a weird green light, as if I had light bulbs underneath my skin. As I stared, the light started spreading all along my arm, and in just a few seconds my entire body was glowing.

My skin was tingling like there was Apple Fizzplosion running through my veins – and the light was still getting stronger. Soon my friends were covering their eyes with their hands.

I WAS BRIGHTER THAN THE SUN!

'What's going on?' I heard one of the shadow-guards mutter – and suddenly I knew just what to do!

'IT'S DANGER TIME!' I grinned and held out my palms towards them. Super-awesome bolts of green lightning *pew-pew*'d out of my hands, right into the shadow-guards – and they faded out of existence!

I couldn't believe it. It turns out I had Freaky magic too! I mean, I know I didn't say anything in my letters, but I had secretly been properly jealous of the rest of the gang. I mean, my mates could turn invisible and transform into sharks – all I had was a pencil case with a torch! But as I stood there, glowing like the sun, I remembered that I'd been holding that torch when the crazy lightning struck my house, and I guess, somehow, strange electrical powers had been transferred to me! My magic had just taken a little longer to come along than everyone else's. But it arrived right at the perfect moment!

As soon as the shadows had been blasted away, the light and the tingling in my body faded.

IT HAD BEEN THE BIT OF

FREAKY LUCK WE NEEDED.

We burst into the room where they were keeping Mum's **WEATHER RAY,** and there it was, sitting in a dramatic pool of light.

So we wheeled it back past the cowering guard dogs, under the broken security cameras, through the deactivated laser beams, scooping up the now-normal-hamster-sized Mr Fluffles from the empty canteen, straight past the first security guard, who was still searching for his keys on the floor, and over the drawbridge of terrified, flesh-eating piranhas . . . And, once we were back outside by the bikes,

STEP 4
WAS COMPLETE!

'We did it!' I cheered.

'Yeah, but what's that awful smell?' Suzy asked.

'I think it's coming from the WEATHER RAY.' Eric gagged, almost being sick from the smell.

He was right. There was a funky pong coming from my mum's weather-zapping invention – and Max was about to show us why.

He reached up to a little hatch that said:

WARNING: LASER BEAM. DO NOT TOUCH!
And before I could stop him he'd wiggled his little baby
fingers into the gap and pinged off the cover.

Something fell out and hit the ground with a sloppy

THUD!

and the revolting stink became a hundred times worse!

'Ew! It's a NAPPY!' Jamelia whined.

'A poopy nappy!' Ronnie added.

And, sure enough, the thing that fell out of the **WEATHER
RAY** was one of Max's disgusting poo-catchers.

I remembered what Mum had said earlier to the police
officer – the thing that had caught in my mind, although
I hadn't understood why:

**IT WAS STARTING TO SMELL LIKE
OLD NAPPIES.**

I suddenly had one of those flashbacks like you see in the movies.

It was the night of the Freaky storm. Dad was watching football. Max filled his nappy, then climbed out of his highchair and vanished.

He must have gone into Mum's lab after all.

Ripped off his disgusting, rotten, eggy, poop-filled nappy.

Opened up the hatch that had the words WARNING: LASER BEAM. DO NOT TOUCH *written on it, and . . .*

SHOVED HIS NAPPY <u>INSIDE!</u>

My brother's pooey nappy must have sloshed around the inner workings of Mum's invention. I bet that's what that weird BUZZING sound was . . .

Now, I'm no scientist, but even I know that having a big pile of baby poo inside a highly unstable invention designed to control the weather with NO LIMITER installed is a recipe for disaster!

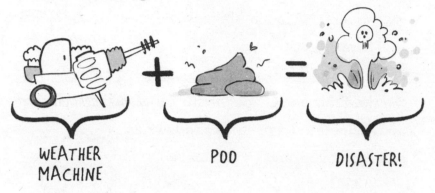

WEATHER MACHINE + POO = DISASTER!

I suddenly remember the door to the lab flying open, and realize that it wasn't the storm blasting INTO our house. It was Mum's invention overloading and **BLASTING** *a laser beam of nappy-infused, toxic weather energy OUT through the pointy end of the telescope bit, smashing STRAIGHT THROUGH THE WINDOW, and into the sky over Freaky.*

I SNAPPED OUT OF MY FLASHBACK.

'So it was YOU that started the Freaky storm!' I said in amazement to Max, who was smiling at his nine-month-old poopy nappy like he'd been reunited with an old friend. 'You and Mum's invention! That's what gave us all these freaky abilities and made all the weird stuff happen . . .'

'So does that mean your mum can zap these powers away? Because I'd really like to have a bath,' Eric said, and we all laughed.

Before we could high-five each other, there was a screech of brakes and a white Shadow-Tech van skidded into the car park. THE SAME VAN THAT HAD BEEN AT MY SCHOOL!

That was when Max blew our cover and started crying like a baby. I know he IS a baby, but there's a time and a place to act like one, and hiding in the bushes from an evil shadow-agent is NOT one of them. I passed him over to Ronnie the baby-whisperer to try to shush him, but it was too late!

THIS WAS IT.

WE ALL THOUGHT IT.

OUR TIME WAS <u>UP</u>.

THERE WAS NO WAY WE WERE GETTING OUT OF <u>THIS ONE.</u>

That was when you took hold of my hand. You must have lost your balance or gone light-headed or something, because you started leaning towards me and your eyes closed like this . . .

But luckily, before your face bumped into mine, we were hit with the intense beam of searchlights from a helicopter overhead, which seemed to snap you back to your senses.

FREEZE! YOU'RE UNDER ARREST!

In the glare of the searchlights, we all watched a super-awesome secret agent abseil out of the chopper and do some incredible kung-fu moves on the Shadow-Tech guy, before he put him in handcuffs and arrested him.

He looked so super awesome that it was like watching the real-life Zack Danger right before our eyes. Which is why it was such a SHOCK when he took his cool secret-agent shades off and I SAW THAT . . .

IT WAS MY DAD!!!

OF ALL THE FREAKY THINGS
TO HAPPEN TO ME THIS YEAR,
THAT WAS THE **FREAKIEST**.

'But – but I thought you were a rubbish musician?!'
I stammered.

'That's just my cover. I'm a secret agent, and I've been spying on Shadow Tech for years. Your mum was right that they were **TROUBLE** and **NOT TO BE TRUSTED**, and finally, thanks to you, we have proof!'

I guess that explains why he's SO useless at most other things in life. It's all just 'an act'. I mean, if he was super awesome all the time, then people would guess that he was a secret agent, so he *pretends* to be

THE WORLD'S MOST EMBARRASSINGLY USELESS DAD

so it doesn't blow his cover.

SMART, DAD. REALLY SMART!

It turns out Dad's man cave (our basement) wasn't really a man cave either. It was his super-secret spy base! Dad said that his notepads full of awful song lyrics are really full of **TOP-SECRET** government files and the disgusting brown armchair that was chewed up by our old dog (RIP, Billy) has an actual ejector seat. Even his wedding ring doubles as a spy camera! How crazy is that?!

And remember how, the morning after the storm, our house was weirdly back to normal again . . . ?

'Ah, well, I could hardly let your mum come home to find the house half destroyed while I was meant to be in charge! So I pulled a few strings and called in the super-spy top-secret clean-up crew for an emergency mission – Operation: Clean Up Dad's Mess! By the time your mum got home, it was sparkling. She didn't notice a thing!' Dad explained with a wink.

'Of course, once I realized that Shadow Tech were shadowing you, and that the Danger Gang were ON TO those evil shadow-agents, we decided to let you make your way to Shadow Tech HQ and see if you'd manage to break in . . . which you DID, obviously!

I knew you would. You'll make a great spy one day, just like your dad,' he said proudly, which made me forgive him a little for being pretty irresponsible and knowingly letting his two sons and their schoolfriends try to take on an evil company in the middle of the night. I guess that trusting we'd succeed just makes him an even more

AWESOME SECRET AGENT.

So the police shut down Shadow Tech, and STEP 4 was most definitely COMPLETE – the WEATHER RAY was back in safe hands! All that was left now was . . .

STEP 5: SAY GOODBYE AND RETURN TO FREAKY AS HEROES

I'll never forget my dad lifting the walkie-talkie to his mouth and saying, '*Come in, Jean-Claude. Bring the chopper down – we're ready to go home.*'

'Jean-Claude?' I said, puzzled. 'The French pen pal you told me about?'

'He's my undercover spy partner.' Dad grinned. 'And our ride back to Freaky . . . unless you'd rather ride your bikes?'

'**NO WAY!**' we all cheered.

And so the Danger Gang boarded Dad's spy-chopper.

FIRST STOP WAS YOUR HOUSE!

Saying goodbye was pretty weird with everyone watching, wasn't it? I think I wanted to tell you something, but I wasn't quite sure what to say, so I just did that fist bump, which, looking back now, was a bit lame for two super-spies. SORRY.

And then the rest of the Danger Gang rode back to Freaky in the chopper.

STEP 6: NEVER TELL ANYONE, EVER!

'This is by far the most important part of the plan,' said Dad (the secret agent) on the flight home.

He said it's because he doesn't want another secret evil company getting wind of the **WEATHER RAY** and it falling into the wrong hands again – but I think he's just scared that Mum will discover that he's living a double life as a really cool spy. I don't know why. I mean, if I was her, I would totally have married *Spy-Dad* and not *Out-of-Work-Musician-Dad* who only showers once a week.

We all promised we wouldn't tell another soul about Mum's invention and what it had done (with the help of Max), but somehow it didn't feel enough. I mean, what if news got out about it? What if someone else realized they could use it to zap people into sharks or turn them invisible or into giant pumpkins or shrink them to the size of flying ants? What if someone else stole it? As long as Mum's invention existed, the world was in danger.

IT WAS JUST <u>TOO RISKY!</u>

Then Ronnie Nutbog, of all people, had a very Ronnie Nutbog idea.

'Let's smash it up!' he suggested.

I looked at him. 'But, if we destroy the machine that made everything go weird, then my mum won't be able to reverse it. **WE'LL ALL BE FREAKY FOREVER!'**

But, as those words left my lips, I realized that it wasn't Mum's machine and that storm zapping us that had made us freaky. Freakiness had been inside us all along. All right, we hadn't been transforming into sharks, disappearing or glowing (I kind of think glowing is the MOST AWESOME – am I biased? Maybe I'm biased.) before the **WEATHER RAY** got zapped, but whether it's super obvious or hidden somewhere beneath the surface, one way or another, I guess we're all a little bit freaky.

AND I WOULDN'T CHANGE IT FOR THE WORLD!

So, as we flew over the frozen surface of Lake Freaky, we each placed a hand on the WEATHER RAY and heaved it out of the helicopter door.

We watched it fall and smash through the ice. As it sank, the whole lake began to glow a familiar shade of green underneath the ice and we knew that, while this adventure was nearly over, the Danger Gang was here to stay.

I guess all that's left to say is have a Merry Christmas and a *dangerous* New Year!

OVER AND OUT,

DANGER FRANKY
X

PS That's not a 'kiss'. I accidentally wrote the letter X.

EPILOGUE

So now you know what went down in Freaky. How one stinky storm changed a town and altered the lives of eight kids FOREVER!

Franky never told his mum about her husband's true identity. His dad went on pretending to be useless and annoying, and she went on zapping him with the Husband-o-shhhh on a regular basis, totally oblivious to the fact that he was a super-awesome, top-secret undercover agent.

As for Franky's mum, well, she spent all her free time inventing things you wouldn't even find in your wildest dreams, until one day she called Franky, Dad and Max into the garage – sorry, the *Home Science Lab* – excited to show them her NEW INVENTION.

And so the Danger Gang's adventures were only just beginning. Franky kept writing to his ~~girl~~friend Dani, telling her all about his weird life as things got freakier and freakier – and, rumour has it, the Danger Gang still live in Freaky today, keeping an eye on things, making sure the town's *freakiness* doesn't get out of hand!

So, if you ever fall asleep on the Tube and find yourself just outside London, two stops past Strange, but not quite as far as Bonkers, be sure to keep your eyes peeled for anything out of the ordinary . . .

or YOU might become the next member of

THE DANGER GANG.

FREAKY FOREVER!

THE END

ACKNOWLEDGEMENTS

I would like to start by thanking the dangerously talented Shane Devries for the most ridiculously awesome illustrations. Each time we start a new book I am totally blown away by what you create and on top of that you are a lovely human. Thanks, Shane!

Thanks to my editor, Natalie Doherty – you have taught me more about writing than anyone. Without you, these books would be, well, let's be honest, a total mess! Thank you.

Huge thanks to the whole team at Penguin Random House – you really are a Danger Gang for daring to believe in me and my work, and I can't thank you enough for it!

Thanks to the design, editorial and production gang: Emily Smyth, Mandy Norman, Wendy Shakespeare,

Jane Tait, Marcus Fletcher, Pippa Shaw and Eliza Walsh.

Thanks to Sarah Roscoe, Geraldine McBride, Kat Baker, Rozzie Todd, Sophie Marston, Eleanor Rhodes-Davies, Toni Budden, Becki Wells, Karin Burnik, Lorraine Levis and everyone in sales.

Thanks to the whole rights gang, Zosia Knopp, Anne Bowman, Maeve Banham, Susanne Evans, Lena Petzke and Beth Fennell, and to Harriet Venn, Sophia Dryden and Lottie Halstead in PR and marketing.

And, of course, thanks to Tom Weldon, Francesca Dow and Amanda Punter. Without you, my stories would only be read by my parents.

Thanks to the most unique and brilliant manager on the planet, Fletch. Thanks for not only giving me my entire career but being a great friend to share it with. Your belief can make dinosaurs fly.

Huge thanks to my literary agent, Stephanie Thwaites, for being the first to really see potential in my stories and making all this happen, and everyone at Curtis Brown.

Thanks to Kaz Gill and the team at Statham Gill Davies.

Thanks to Rachel Drake, Nikki Garner, Tommy Jay Smith and David Spearing, for always going above and beyond for me.

Thanks to Lou and Susana, for everything you do at home so I can actually get some words written between the chaos!

Thanks to my own gang: Danny, Dougie and Harry. It's good to be back.

To my family, Mum, Dad and Carrie for the support, love and life you've given me.

To my wife, Giovanna – there aren't enough pages in the world for me to write the thanks you deserve. I love you.

To my three boys, Buzz, Buddy and Max – you are the ultimate Danger Gang.

Finally, to you, the reader, for using your mind to make sense of my words. I hope you enjoyed them.

SPOT THE DIFFERENCE

BEFORE THE STORM

Dad's super-spy top-secret clean-up crew did an awesome job of tidying up **MUM'S HOME SCIENCE LAB** after the Freaky storm – but they got a few things wrong! Can you spot the **FIVE** differences between these before and after pictures?

(The labels on the left will help you find the differences. Answers at the bottom of the page.)

AFTER THE STORM

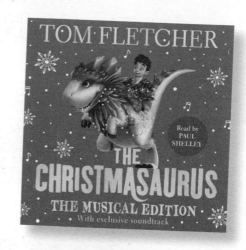

Join William on his next adventure . . .

THE CHRISTMASAURUS AND THE WINTER WITCH

the magical smash hit from number-one bestselling author

TOM FLETCHER

Illustrated by SHANE DEVRIES

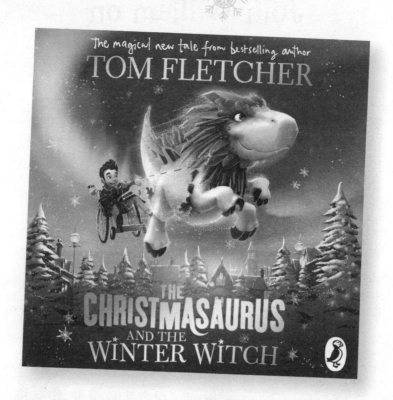

Have you ever wondered what's really under your bed . . . ?

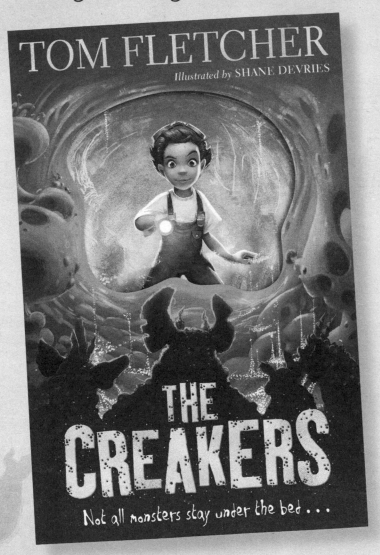

TOM FLETCHER

Illustrated by SHANE DEVRIES

THE CREAKERS

Not all monsters stay under the bed . . .

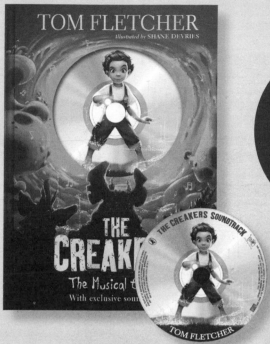

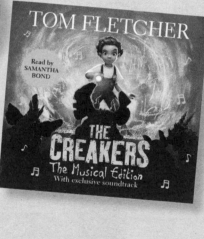